Stephen Conroy has lived his entire life in the Capital Region in Upstate New York and is proud to produce his first published book, while incorporating some local ties within the story. He is married and has two young daughters with his wife, Nicole. The story started forming listening to his dad tell campfire stories on their summer vacations to help lead the development of this story.

To my amazing wife, Nicole, I thank you for all of your love and support and I love you dearly. Thank you to my dad (Stephen Conroy) as well, who concocted the greatest camp fire story of all time and you are greatly missed every day. To my mother, Robin Brand, I just simply cannot state enough how thankful I am for everything you do and your continuous support and love. Thank you to all of my family.

Stephen Conroy

PANIC THROUGH THE PINES

AUSTIN MACAULEY PUBLISHERS™

LONDON • CAMBRIDGE • NEW YORK • SHARJAH

Ordering Information
Quantity sales: Special discounts are available on quantity purchases by corporations, associations, and others. For details, contact the publisher at the address below.

Publisher's Cataloging-in-Publication data
Conroy, Stephen
Panic Through the Pines

ISBN 9781649792198 (Paperback)
ISBN 9781649792204 (ePub e-book)

Library of Congress Control Number: 2021904323

www.austinmacauley.com/us

First Published 2021
Austin Macauley Publishers LLC
40 Wall Street, 33rd Floor, Suite 3302
New York, NY 10005
USA

mail-usa@austinmacauley.com
+1 (646) 5125767

Thanks to Austin Macauley Publishers for guiding me on each and every step of publishing.

Chapter 1
Lake Life

A nice, quiet morning on the deck of the camp located in Chestertown around Loon Lake about an hour north of Albany, New York was the winter and summer break I always knew I needed. It was a peaceful place that was purchased by my grandparents back in the seventies and had been used by the Marshall family tree for the last several decades. My grandparents were hard working people with only one child, my grandfather was a WWII veteran and a mail carrier and my grandmother was a legal aid for a prominent attorney in the Albany area and lived in a cozy three-bedroom house in the small town of Cohoes and saved and saved enough to be able to afford the house they lived in and also made the decision instead of taking weekly trips elsewhere they would venture to the north. They enjoyed taking scenic drives to the North Country when my dad was a little boy and one drive took them to the small town of Chestertown and they fell in love with the atmosphere. They would stay as renters at a local motel for a few days here and there and then started looking into renting a camp for a week and after a while of doing that they started having serious discussions at whichever camp they happened to be renting about being able to pull off a purchase of a property.

There were two most common ways to go about this; one did they want to purchase land and build their own place or contract it out to have it built in a year or so depending on weather, two was to purchase an already built structure, which you would wonder why would anyone sell at this magical place. People sell houses all the time for a wide array of reasons; death, money issues, less appealing than one may have originally thought about maintaining the upkeep of the property year round, who knows? They kept both options on the table as to not pigeon hole themselves. The stars aligned on their visit at the end of the summer in 1972 and gave them their opportunity. They were doing their usual walk around the camp village inside the white pillars when they happened to notice a for sale sign at the top of a driveway. They ventured down to the camp and started to peak around the place. It didn't appear as if anyone was home so they took a little trip around back and saw the lake and deck and fell in love. On the for-sale sign was a phone number that they hurriedly jotted down and almost ran back to the camp they were renting to get on the rotary phone and almost had to make the call three times because they were trying to dial too fast. My grandmother was pacing the living room right next to where my grandfather was making the call holding onto her rosary beads praying to John and Mary that someone would answer the phone.

"Good morning, Dick Perkins, how can I help you?"

My grandfather blurted out, "Yes, Yes, I'm calling about the property by the lake. My wife and I would like to see the inside and we are very interested in purchasing the property."

A log cabin looking property that was painted brown with a front door that was fire engine red come to find out the owner who purchased the land and just had the property built three years ago died suddenly of heart failure and the party handling the estate did not wish to keep the property, best of both worlds; the camp was almost brand spanking new and had hardly been used and as my grandparents almost always said still smelled the freshness of the wood the first couple of summers there. Plus, something that they never really imagined and only dreamed about was *lakeside* property, this was a home run. Loon Lake, I always found it a peculiar name but came to find out it is in fact a type of bird and they just happened to be prevalent in this area; hence, the name. My dad would always joke that they named it that way after the Marshall clan bought their property.

They would save whatever allotted vacation time they were given and take off in the summer when my dad was out of school and then when they were able to escape for a long weekend, they never missed an opportunity. Entering the small little community of camps was always one of my biggest excitements, it signaled the start of relaxation and fun and family time. You would have a relatively short drive, usually no more than an hour unless the driver wanted to view some scenery before getting to the camp, after getting off the highway exit a left-hand turn would start you on the path through the small town and eventually, the lake would appear to enter our small little village of camps a casual right onto a dirt road and at the entrance on either side where these two white pillars, and wow, were they great to see. Then a slight veer left brought you closer to the lakeside camps and that's where the Marshall Camp was located, just down that road probably no more than a mile past the pillars.

Property values were at the time relatively decent priced, not exactly cheap but if we listed the cabin now in this market, we would be looking at a huge profit with camps and lakeside properties going for three-four hundred thousand dollars if not more depending on updating and space etc. In between sports seasons was how our weeks were allotted once I got older. When I was younger, staying there for three weeks in the summer time was amazing and relaxing. The sounds of the motor boats on the water, swimming, playing king of the dock, eating hamburgers and hot dogs on the deck, then capping the night off with a fire and either a game or some corny scary story or history lesson. We would rent the camp out when none of the family would want to use it, which provided some extra income. But having memories in a place like this so often is why you wouldn't entertain selling in any market, the fun memories are far more valuable than the price my grandparents or parents could have fetched for such a small piece of heaven at the base of the Adirondacks.

We lucked out because the camps surrounding us were pretty similar family structures, decent size, kids, and located within New York state, so schooling schedules were similar from time to time; depending on schedules, some of the other families would not be there at exactly the same time but it's not like that's all we did was rely on other families being there. It helped for games of capture the flag and hide and go seek and king of the dock in the lake or judging who had the best launch off the rope swing into the lake. Our camp was not huge but the lakeside view and deck was perfect. Four bedrooms with *just* enough room for a bed and a tiny dresser to put your clothes for the current visit in and to have whoever was going to make a guest appearance, either for a night or longer from the family. Even though my dad was an only child, my grandfather had two siblings and my grandmother had three siblings that all had children, so there was an ample amount of relatively close family to choose from to spend time at the camp with. A sign carefully placed just to the right of the front door after coming down the driveway is a hand-crafted wooden nameplate, Marshall. My grandfather waddled it himself on one of the first trips to the camp after purchasing it with my grandmother. James was his name and as was my dad's and my name also made it pretty simple at family gatherings that you would at least get someone's attention usually only after two James's unless it was a little bit sterner tone from my mom or grandmother. The first day we would get to the camp would always be grocery day at the local Grand Union and set up shop day. We would usually shop in town because the cars were full of bodies and luggage depending on the length of stay and for food preservation purposes. In the late '80s, I was pretty young just being born in 1981 but the parties roared with the family and the Budweiser and burgers were flying into the wee hours. My parents blessed me with a lake time partner in crime, Zach born just two short years after me so I was all set; had my king of the dock opponent or tag team partner, depending if there were other so-called challengers that would try and knock us off our throne. We both played multiple sports growing up but Zach was the intellectual one for sure always excelling in school. We would have the usual brother-brother fights growing up, someone stole the other's toy or so and so cheated at *war* but we always had each other's back when it came to an aggressive game of basketball or king of the dock match with other kids. We always likened ourselves to a dominant tag team partner like we would watch in the W.W.F. on weekend mornings and vowed to remain that way even through tough times when we got older. I remember my goal was to always try to stay awake for Saturday Night Live, this was in my opinion the peak of the show of the late '80s and into the '90s with stars such as Chris Farley and Adam Sandler taking over from the previous stars of the like Chevy Chase and Steve Martin and passing to newcomers like Will Farrell, Tina Fey, and Jimmy Fallon, just to name a few. You would always underestimate the toll swimming and running and hiking through the woods and eating goober grape sandwiches would take such a toll and staying up usually never happened. No worries, that's when it shifted to adult time, which, let's be honest, is needed depending on how many kids were present on the given day and it was their escape from the everyday struggle of life and their vacation also.

There were two public beaches that we would frequent if we wanted some interaction with other families, one in particular was not more than a ten minute walk and had a small docking station for boats a nice dock to get a running start to run into the lake and a dock not that far out in the water once we were a little bit older to swim out to and sit and catch some rays or watch the water skiers and tubers go by and quietly root for them to wipe out when the driver would take a turn to fast and the person would go flying over the wake sometimes head over feet or watching the tube flip and fling them in the air like we were shooing mosquitoes away during the nighttime fire. The other beach, we did not frequent as much because we would actually have to drive there and when you look at all the shit, we would have to pack in the car just taking a stroll down the road with our cooler and station wagon with all the daily necessities was just plain easier, plus, it usually was more busy as it was roadside so it attracted more people from around the area where the smaller one was really just of families who were staying at camps nearby. The lake itself was not massive but it provided enough of a radius for a scenic walk or car ride and even better when the family on occasion would rent a boat; a great boat ride.

The wood for the campfire was usually dropped off by the same local man that would sell it to us pretty cheap by the yard because we would buy enough to last the week or weeks barring any rain at night, which we would then just have a day time fire, nothing wrong with that, all is good on Lake Time! Happy hour, fire time, eating time, you name it. There were rain activities in place to pass the time, a small TV with four channels was in the living room or a puzzle could be had or a card game, solitaire for the alone time, poker to scratch the gambling itch with pennies, or a classic for me and my bro war, flip a card, whoever is higher takes the card, flip the same number or royalty at the same time have a war, lay three cards down, then the next one, same thing whoever lays down the highest card takes the whole pot and you would not know the excitement of the ever so rare double war. Simple game to pass some time hoping the rain would stop. We would visit a few of the local golf courses on our extended stays and have some fun with dad and grandpa losing golf balls in the woods. We would rent a motorboat from the lakes lone marina from time to time for either a day rental or a few days here and there to get some water sports in or a different fishing spot, we did have a dock at the camp that we could have stored a boat during our stays but my grandparents were fine; just keeping a few kayaks stationed there and with our own dock and the beaches near by the water experience was just fine.

There is a great local restaurant that had the best chicken parm when we wanted to treat ourselves or no one felt like cooking called the Laketime Restaurant that specializes in all types of American fare as well as mentioned before an amazing chicken parm if you wanted a break from the usual burger, but they did an amazing pizza and wing special that offered guests a nice take out option if the nightly grill session was getting rained out and turning on the oven was out of the question…Sure, traveling elsewhere would have been more luxurious, maybe on an airplane to Disney or a cruise; sure, more extravagant but again the sights and sounds of the lake life proved to be perfect for my family. As everyone grew older and families became more busy, the stays shortened and the crowd was smaller as family members pass or other families in surrounding camps get busy with their lives and their children move away but the feeling always remained whenever we would return there no matter with who or for how long because the memories had been cemented for decades of week visits and weekends with family and friends. It's a lot of time for stories to be kept by the Marshall crew and any new extended family that joined for the ride.

You became part of the local club when you owned a camp which, I guess, was similar to a homeowners' association, general upkeep of the camp and rent to upstanding people that would not trash the camp or the grounds in general and it was kind of click-y who owned what, how long had they had been there, how big was their camp, where were they from, how much money did they have. My grandparents didn't indulge in any of that, they kept the camp in pristine condition and their tax check cleared just fine when it was presented for payment by the town clerk. Some residents soaked up being on the lake charter. I guess it gave them a sense of power and entitlement that they were more important than other camp owners and looking for a pinecone that may have been out of place in a driveway or the fire went a little too high the night before. My grandfather would always joke and run and grab us if we were there together and say, "Alright, boys, best behavior; here comes the pinecone police, straighten up."

He understood what the overall purpose was to keep the grounds clean and we abided by that because we were upstanding people and I guess in some instances owners and visitors would take that for granted and not show quite the same level of respect but that didn't mean we couldn't poke a little fun at their expense.

Chapter 2
Legend Has It

Walking the grounds of our camp village was always exciting; especially in the summertime, there was always a special buzz in the air, warmer weather, families laughing at the beach; but the wintertime hikes provided a unique perspective as well, the beauty of the falling snow and the glistening on the frozen lake, we would always stroll past one camp in particular that was heavily wooded and not well seen from the road through the tall pines. This was a walk that my dad took with his dad all of the time and where a story started, that was then passed down to me through these very same walks and at the nightly fire or inside in the living room during a thunderstorm at night when the TV connection would be lost and if you ask me, they were both equally terrifying; you would either hear an unknown sound crackling in the woods or an unexpected break of a piece of firewood collapsing in the fire pit or a loud boom of thunder at just the most perfect time in the story. The camps were all numbered really; eventually just for incoming visitors and anyone who actually made a camp their mailing address' sake but mailboxes lined the entrance just before the two white pillars welcoming visitors. Nailed to a tree at the start of the driveway of this camp, I always remembered two white numbers 33. I would always try to yell out the camp numbers when we would walk; it was our lake version of I spy because as you could imagine some of the numbers, depending on where the owner decided to place them were not exactly the easiest to view, not like strolling your neighborhood at home with limited visual impairments. My grandfather knew the couple who bought the camp within a few years around the same time he and my grandmother bought the Marshall Camp, a nice couple with one son who was a few years younger than my dad, overall, he would always say they were pretty nice in passing and if their beach times synchronized, they would exchange pleasantries and the two boys would jump off the dock or gather a group of other kids for a game of volleyball. The camp from my dad's recollection was usually maintained from a landscaping point and was usually in fair condition from their walks by when he was younger, not that they ever went there physically since everyone usually retreated back to their own personal camps after a long day of water and beach activities. My dad remembered their vacations lined up in the summer for several years in a row after learning from Pappa they were New Yorkers; also just a few hours south of Albany, so were on a similar schooling schedule.

Then one random summer when the Marshall's made their usual last trip up in August for the week, the other family was nowhere to be found. My dad believes it was right around when he was maybe fourteen or fifteen, but my dad played sports and I guess they just figured that the other young boy was involved in sports, also, or they were unable to leave the family business at the time, which my grandfather learned was a small bakery in Poughkeepsie and they just never thought any more of it since going to the camp every year, it was nice sometimes to connect with familiar faces but with a high renter population, this was not always the norm, families would change week to week over the course of each summer. Our walks would always continue and the rumors would swirl through the village as the camp on our walk got more wooded and secluded seemingly by the summer. No one recalled seeing a for sale sign ever posted, which never really means that a sale didn't take place or the family gave the camp away due to death and the son being too young to be able or have the means to care for the property, maybe the family's bakery was struggling to make ends meet and had to close up shop. Each lap by the camp produced a different take or a different possibility that someone heard something from someone while drinking the day away at the beach about whatever happened. There would be lights on from time to time before the camp became so obscure behind the trees that the light faded over the next few years, just like the memory of them playing volleyball or basketball when a basketball hoop was installed by a family who lived near the beach that would allow other children and people to use it.

A prevailing theory is that there was a fire at the families' bakery while the mom, dad, and young boy were all working and that the only one who survived was the boy but barely with severe third degree burns that required multiple surgeries and left the right side of his face misconfigured and deformed. Also being at the presumed time my dad was only again fourteen or fifteen, so this boy would have been slightly younger around eleven or twelve, and would have needed to be placed in foster care after the lengthy hospital stay, which almost served as his first actual foster home with nurses and doctors providing potential and support. My dad took the theory and ran with it developing his own version of what could have potentially happened next because it did look like at least from one of his last memories there was slight activity at the camp when he got, older which would make the son older and able to assume the property once he reached legal age.

He formed the story around the fire and accident and how badly the boy was injured and how deformed he was from injuries from the terrible fire. Spending years in foster homes until reaching the legal age to be able to live independently on his own, which, at the time, in New York State, was seventeen before heading to the lake to spend the rest of his days living alone and in isolation away from all the people that cast judgment and cast horrified looks as he would try and go out in public and live a decent normal lifestyle, which, after countless trips out in public and trying, he was broken and retreated to a life of isolation. Winters inside, walking through the trails and taking advantage of less traffic and less visual exposure. Summertime, on the other hand, was when my dad said he really loathed for a multitude of reasons one of the main ones was just like my family heading to the camp to enjoy a week or longer of fun family activities and laughter, a rage, and jealousy grew with each laughing child by the fire night after night. This is usually the point in the story where my dad would shift to the front of his chair or tree stump, he happened to be sitting on around the fire. One beautiful summer night in July, the lake was booming with families,

21

enjoying the Fourth of July activities with the smell of BBQs and the sounds of motorboats and fireworks at night he *snapped*. He couldn't take it any longer and ventured out from his secluded camp and stood in the tree line surrounding his property, waiting patiently for the next sound to trigger his anger (sounds of laughter) from about a few hundred feet away from his property, he darted through the trees like he was a huntsman with one distinct purpose in mind but unlike a hunter looking for his next meal, this tormented individual had one goal "End the laughter," and like the sounds of the fireworks exploding the man secretly finding a discreet path to the sounds he heard since he re-learned them from his winter off-path adventures to emerge and deliver such forceful blows to his victims to end the laughs one at a time. My dad would usually make a swinging motion and say, "Boom," loudly at the perfect time for effect, causing anyone present to jump or scream.

The first time was pretty sloppy as it was just anger and rage, causing the destruction of maybe a family that owned the actual camp or a family that was just looking to escape the everyday grind in a family safe setting. Like a baker honing his craft, he developed tactics and a skillfulness that developed each time; a laughter or a potential family enjoying a visit or him, even now craving the excitement going out and taking action against those who made his upbringing so miserable and cast him aside, like a detriment to society but he would receive the ultimate payback unleashing his rage and fury over the ones enjoying what he was robbed of in his young youth. The weapon was unknown but authorities and per my dad was never found but believed to be a club like object from the coroners and police reports of blunt force trauma usually to the head.

This story, during fire time, was usually a classic, because my dad would always warn us to be careful where we would venture into the woods to get small sticks for kindling the fire and would always remind us of the terror that the lake legend caused and that he could still be at large and still on the hunt for unsuspecting family's, just trying to have a good time. He would usually get the fire started and wait until we were well into the s'more portion of the fire and nice and relaxed and he would venture into the camp for several minutes due to a needed bathroom break that going behind a tree was not an option or he was going to go inside for more snacks, whatever he could drum up at the exact time. Several minutes would pass and he still would be "inside" the camp; all in the meantime he would be sneaking around the camp outside on a tiny path through the trees and when we were not looking, he would jump out of the woods and scream, "Boom," which I would give him credit, even though as we would get older, he always timed it perfectly and there would always be chips, marshmallows, whatever we were snacking on thrown all over the place, as well as several yelps and screams. I'm pretty sure that one time when he did this, we were maybe six or seven years old and we had one of the neighbor's kids over to hang out by the fire and when he jumped out of the woods the kid pissed his pants, he got a pretty stern talking to and the child would come over for a fire again but we knew we weren't getting the legend story that night and we would always chuckle when the kid left the fire area for a few moments for an actual bathroom break or was summoned back to his residence for the evening.

Chapter 3
The Trifecta

It was a fairly normal Tuesday afternoon a week after Christmas, the sun was out and I finished my shift at the bank and headed to Cohoes for a visit with my dad. I was trying to make them as frequent as possible as the forecast was bleak and I was trying to squeeze every last possible moment. A lung cancer diagnosis about one year and a half earlier for my dad really put a damper on the hopes of the excitement and building an adult relationship for many years to come. So Tuesday afternoons became even as special as a Sunday dinner would be. His spirits were pretty strong throughout treatment amid the overall negative diagnosis. Really, at that point, what else can do you, pray, hope for a miracle treatment. Unfortunately, treatment and cures for this horrible disease have been elusive for minds way smarter than mine. Being the number one cancer killer in men, we will hope someday through research and development we will finally get there. Not to say my dad is completely innocent. He was a smoker for some time. I remember our younger days and the Grand Union trips down the hill that usually included a stop at the customer service desk to purchase a carton of Marlboro Reds. A lot of people who continue to smoke have not gotten lung cancer, he even *quit* and at the time of the diagnosis, he hadn't had a cigarette in ten years so yeah, I was pissed off. I've read that over the course of time in years that the lungs will recuperate and build back to strength and normalcy after that kind of time period after quitting smoking. But second opinions still sometimes will not reverse the bleakness and darkness that lies ahead. We would still be able to take lake trips but with him sick now, the stays were shorter and my grandfather now the only one alive from the dynamic duo he and my grandmother formed getting older and unable to care for the camp, they would hire someone to take care of the property, snow removal, any maintenance needs to, but the talk already started about plans of passing it down relatively soon and expedited even quicker with my dad's health now in question, Zach and I became the blessed two to carry on the legacy.

Dad was in the living room as usual so pretty standard operation so far and at the time of cell phone development instant access to news was still a little behind. I'm pretty sure my dad read it in the newspaper. I don't know maybe it made the local 6 p.m. news. He asked with hope that it wasn't in fact my friend who had been in the accident while working snow removal. I hadn't heard anything of the sort so kind of assumed maybe he misread the name or thought my friends name was something different. I actually think the overall visit with my dad went pretty well that day. I don't recall the topics we covered and sometimes just sitting in the room watching some afternoon television was all I needed. Well over the course of the next few days, I surely wished that it was not actually my friend. I'm pretty sure it

26

was a phone call, maybe a text honestly, it is still pretty fuzzy for me on exactly I found out it was Kevin that had in fact been involved in some sort of accident that placed him in an I.C.U. room at Albany Medical Center in a coma. I guess I had been pretty lucky but showing up to a hospital and seeing a group of your peers at 24-25 years grieving and hoping for a miraculous recovery of someone that had a lifetime of memories and life to live. He was a childhood friend and someone I truly looked up to, he was a good athlete, baseball, basketball, soccer. "Cool as the other side of the pillow," Stu Scott voice. I was the best man at his wedding; even after as you grew up, you may not connect as often with people you used to but when we did a beat was not missed no matter how long it had been between visits. Now looking at his current state unresponsive lying helpless with grieving family and friends by his side and in the waiting area was not how I envisioned one of our visits going at this point in our lives.

Now the next part, I vividly remember receiving a phone call from Kevin's sister delivering the news that Kevin had passed away. Back to fuzziness because I just remember being in shock and not being able to form any words. "I hope," I at least said. I was sorry for the family's loss but I just needed to get to where they were and be there for them. One of the memories that I carry with me is in junior year of high school we had quite a few friends working at the local Burger Shack and one shift my dad showed up and asked if I could be excused from my shift from the manager, Kevin's dad at the time, and he informed me that my grandmother had passed away that day. So after consoling at my grandparent's house, I took the car back home to shower off the burger smell. Who shows up? Kevin to check in on me to see if I was okay. We spent a lot of time with my grandparents, so he knew them pretty well, going to the mall together, even a few baseball games, and spending some weeks at the camp, he helped Zach and I form a pretty dominant sports team that would dominate at the lake, volleyball, basketball, and king of the dock we were unstoppable. That was a gesture looking back at now I am in awe of and part of what I admired most. Parents burying a child, a wife burying a husband, sisters burying their little brother, young children losing their father. He served in the marine's corp. and is buried in the Gerald B.H. Solomon Saratoga National Cemetery, which I just made my first visit back to after eleven years since the last time I had been there. I am not sure what took me so long to do this and really not sure what brought me there, maybe because it was Memorial Day weekend and not that is when you should only honor a veteran or I just realized, *Wow*, after the services, I hadn't been back since that day and didn't feel like that was right. I finally said, "Thank you and I love you."

Not much more than a few weeks later, the grief and sadness returned or even just continued. My dad was on hospice at home care being tended to and being kept comfortable. I don't recall the day of the week, but the date of January 28th was awful watching my dad pass away. You can know the outcome of a movie but still be overcome by anger, grief, sadness unlike any other. I was ready for 2008, I really was I felt I secured a good job with room to grow and was excited to build on relationships with friends who were in similar positions in their life but to also to deepen relationships within family, you name it, but I was hopeful and excited for all of this. The summer before he passed, we tried to get as much golf in together as we possibly could, because sadly enough, I think we both saw the sad writing on the wall that we more than likely were not going to get another summer together. I was actually able to still play golf with my dad at Frear Park, even while he was receiving chemo. This mother trucker was still shooting 42 for nine holes. I kid you not one mid-morning, we played the front nine literally less than two hours after a chemo treatment he shot a 42, I wish I kept the scorecard but I remember it so clear, he just swung so easy and hit the ball so straight and drained his putts. I couldn't believe it but I was just so happy I mean I never card that low but to be out there playing golf with him it felt like walking up the 18th fairway of Augusta National with a four shot lead and piping your drive down the middle of the fairway, knowing that in a short time, you will be having last year's champion, placing *your* very own green jacket on. This feeling comes back when I am strolling the local golf courses, whether with people I know, a random two or foursome, and regardless of my score. I am not going to the P.G.A. Tour, I wish, but the memory of playing a great game and knowing what I talk to him about now and all of my new life events doesn't end. I envisioned myself enjoying family life at one point down my life's road' uncertain when that time would finally come but hopeful and being stripped to be able to enjoy those moments without him present was an empty feeling.

During that N.F.L. season, family tailgate parties became a tradition, fried turkey and New York Football Giants at my aunt and uncle's house. Wasn't anything out of the ordinary or special about the Giants that year but they made the playoffs. They won the first game, they won the second game, they beat Green Bay in Green Bay when it was negative a million and Tom Coughlin's face looked like it was frozen. Having two weeks before the Giants would play the unbeaten Patriots, that year was spent at my dad's services. I haven't been to a ton of wakes, I guess that is a small blessing but a lesson as you get older will become a more frequent event. I never saw so many people for a service, I didn't sit for more than two minutes as the troves of people just kept coming to pay respect. Location for the big game, where the family party was going to be, we had to do it; regardless even if the Pats won by 40, it would be a welcomed break from the grief. My cousin's house was determined to be the place and he even went and bought a new TV for the event. You will not believe this, I don't think, but before the game, my cousin whipped up a Super Bowl Square pool and everyone jumped in for maybe $5 life-changing money, I know. We had one square left empty and dedicated to putting my dad's name in there. Guess what square hit in the first quarter? Yup, you got it, the square with my dad's name. Even better guess, who won the rest of the squares? Me! And the Giants won the fucking Super Bowl. There was the play of the game where David Tyree caught the ball on his helmet with a defender basically in his jersey with him that I am certain the whole house shook. It gives me chills, we high fived each other, yelled, laughed, ate a ton; it was truly a great moment with family. We knew where his ashes were going to be placed; at the Marshall Camp on a nice spot on the mantle in the main room. I would try my best to keep the story of the legend at the lake going but I just couldn't nail the delivery quite like he did, he was an amazing storyteller and it showed how many times he told the story still brought fear into our hearts when he told it.

Two patriarchal figures gone, representing different stages of life in two months, and well, the saying that deaths or bad things happen in threes. Here we go again, my grandfather was admitted to Albany Medical Center with a grim diagnosis; cancer starting to spread like wildfire through his body. At his age, treatment was risky and chances of recovery were very slim. Eighty years old is a good life, but more about this man; he was almost like another father for me and Zach and my cousin on my mom's side. Hockey trips to all over the north-east, shopping trips for back to school clothes, birthday dinners out. He was transported to Samaritan Hospital after a three week stay in I.C.U., to where he was placed under Hospice care. We left the room he was in for a walk down the hallway to stretch the legs, maybe get some water or a soda. He took that opportunity to finally rest easy. Trying to console your brother moments after telling him that Grandpa was gone. I couldn't believe it, I guess it sounds selfish but I could *not* believe it. Call into work for the weekend again. It was Memorial Day weekend and a traditional camping weekend with friends up in Lake George. Instead, it was wake and funeral time. We watched sports together, he loved baseball and he would always take me to the batting cages to hone my craft. He probably started my love of watching *Sports Center*, we would watch it for hours for highlights and the witty punchlines from the anchors. He particularly loved Chris Berman doing baseball highlights because he would nickname baseball players one of our favorites was Eddie Eat Drink and be Murray (Merry), get it? Again, we knew right where his ashes would be kept but we did not like the new trend on how the mantle at the camp was now using its space for. At least they would be enjoying the space together at a place they both loved so much.

We went to the movies a lot and saw what I consider all the classics of the '90s but a memory I will never forget is just him and I wanted to see *Saving Private Ryan* in 1998, not exactly sure why we were going to see that particular film but in the first ten minutes of the film starting, I now knew why he wanted to see it. I am not sure if you have seen the film. I surely hope you have. I will think a little less of you if you have not. Right off the bat, storming the beaches scene. I don't know what prompted me to but I just happened to glance to my left and noticed a tear strolling down his face. He served in the navy during WWII, so instead of me watching like it was a history lesson, *he lived it*. I couldn't believe he was gone. I felt like a boxer who just got punched in the face and was trying to collect my gatherings, I believe the term may be "punch drunk"? I don't know, what I did know was five fucking months and this was going to be my third funeral service not just of people that, meh, maybe, met a few times, the kind of show up, show support, and get outta dodge. January to May was a blur. In the stages of grief, time is important and everyone goes through them at different speeds and not even in an exact order. Well, newsflash, five months ain't enough time to go through any of 'em. I depended on these people, I needed these people and I was genuinely excited for 2008. Talk about shit getting turned upside down, backwards, crooked, you name it. I guess there's a bible verse somewhere or a religious saying that maybe God will give you a test or challenge that an individual cannot handle. Sadly, whether or not I wanted the test, it was upon me like a pop quiz in chemistry or math class.

These were all people that made lake life so special in some capacity or another. My grandfather bought the place and kept it in our family, my dad brought us there every summer and the bonding with my brother and I were immeasurable. Kevin would actually come to the camp from time to time as we got older and stay with us for the week so three generations of lake ties and memories were now just that, memories, and everything I would do at the lake from that time forward would be without all three of them, a pretty empty feeling and realizing that some of the most important people helped make the camp feel like the most important place in our little world were now gone in the blink of an eye, a blur, snap of the fingers.

Chapter 4
Banking Breakthrough

Walking into the interview, I was extremely excited for a job interview for a bank. For being in my mid-twenties, bouncing around different jobs in retail markets and warehouses, this offered great potential. Even if it was just a teller position. Money hours and handling, well, money, even though you had no rights to it, right, who doesn't like those two things? Noticing the sign on the door of the bank announcing their brand-new hours was a little disheartening; being open from 9 a.m. to 6 p.m., some days, 8 a.m. to 6 p.m., and Saturday hours until 1 p.m. Woof, okay, not the 3 to 4 p.m. I was hoping for but previous jobs included overnights, holidays, weird hours, different shifts, schedule changing week to week. This offered consistency with hopeful room to grow. "Liberty Bank Teller" had a nice ring to it and luckily, I was offered a position, and we were off and running. I completed four years of college, sadly, with no degree to show for it on any level but it checked enough boxes to get in the door on an entry level position, ideally, the love of sports was fit for a gym teacher/coach role but damn, if studying anatomy and physiology with the actual books and not in practice, if ya catch my drift, was a higher priority than we could have a different road but like they say, "Everything happens for a reason."

I was staffed in the Shops of Latham, a fairly busy shopping center just a few miles down the road from Siena College. Although this particular location was city location-wise was pretty strong the building itself was crammed in between a CVS and a locally owned sandwich shop. Win-win for us on both sides selfishly but no drive-through in this particular location so just foot traffic was a little slow but traffic at the A.T.M. was pretty busy and it was a good learning post to learn the banking basics.

One thing I guess I underestimated was the sales culture in the banking industry. Sure you imagine working at a car dealership or a stock investing firm or selling insurance or even real estate. High sales sure, but banking never would have thought. I guess I was just naive that handling customers' money and making sure your drawer matched the totals it should and maybe not get robbed and be financially sound would be enough. And while those were certainly attributes that strongly matter, drawing in new customers with lending options and deposit monies was something that was new to me. But being placed with a pretty cool staff willing to teach and a branch manager that was intelligent and down to earth and offered assistance at every turn was vital to the successful path forward. Even though Jonah Davidson was a Red Sox fan, he also was a Giants' fan and golfer, jackpot, always nice when you strike gold on the sports front to pass the time on the slow banking days, although I'm sure the head teller, Brittany, at the time loved it so much our hour-long sports conversations, ah, well, to each their own, right? It was overall a solid staff and with Jonah and Brittany showing me the ropes and some brief interactions with regional administrators which typically went pretty well, me just trying to be myself and show that I at least had the personality for a future role in a manager position, learning the banking on the go would develop the knowledge base needed. But usually, in my experience, there needs to be a good blend of both, intelligence even isn't just measured by G.P.A. or degrees, although those are pretty strong indicators, don't get me wrong, in an evolving psyche of the ever-changing workforce there needs to be undoubtedly an ability to interact with co-workers and customers to drive success. I have seen both in the drive to different positions. It's a game of either, neither, or both. Obviously, if it's neither the shelf life, nor success rate almost always proves itself, and wonder how one came into the position but no judging from me, they got the job one way or another and did a respectable job in someone's eyes to warrant a specific position.

The bank had an opportunity to move to the end of the plaza and share a building with an incoming burger joint fairly new to the area, which I frequented before at a different location and, man, were they good and gave ya free peanuts when you would stop in. Although Jonah and Brittney were excited for the new location to boost traffic and increase business, which, again, as you know, is important, which leads to greater rewards money-wise with incentives paid out monthly on the manager level. Obviously, the bank had high hopes as well; otherwise, they would not have seized this opportunity. I, on the other hand, was not interested in a long term stay in the one spot. I focused and determined to learn and promote to a different position. The move happened relatively soon after joining the bank, I believe, only about six or seven months after joining as a teller so not exactly a ton of time of service hours in, but again, given the old spot's location, provided ample learning time for the base I would need moving forward. Also talking with other managers and again the same regional managers who were covering the area, I shifted my focus to an assistant manager's position.

This enabled me to travel around to different branch locations and make a name for myself with staff and customers as well. Not minding the travel too much and inconsistency of which particular location I could have been called to if I was more needed elsewhere. I always take away good/bad from anyone customer's or co-workers alike, different views, management style insights from customers about their life; also, I always found interesting. In a lot of instances if you really get to the bottom of a customer face to face interaction, this could be the fifteen to twenty minutes of socialization they have for a day or even longer. Learning to appreciate this and develop a skill set to develop relationships with people that I did not need a bachelor's degree to understand.

I then became an assistant who would cover week vacations or any circumstance where the manager would be out for an extended period of time. Pretty cool feeling to get your feet wet to see the operation and how you would fare in one particular branch, the vacation weeks were pretty simple, work the schedule and keep the ship afloat, but still added responsibility to be the one at the helm, leading the way only if just for a week. Deposits and mortgages, mortgages and deposits. Applications were taken at branch level on good old fashioned legal three copy paper still, opening accounts and transacting was the simple part. Completing an accurate mortgage application was a challenge, at the time, moving from branch to branch was the training and yeah, if it was slow and the manager was still in the office, you would have an opportunity to cover the order and what document was what and why it was needed. There was no real specific, say like classroom training, but you accept whatever the task is and try the best you can and soak up as much info to take to the next stop.

The hours still beat a lot of other jobs that I had recently, even working until 6 p.m., but it let me get to different areas and work with a lot of different customer bases, we specialized in mortgages was the primary focus and it wasn't an investor type style banking, it was relatively small but always ranked high in residential lending, one of the primary money makers for the bank; take in money in the form of deposits at a fair market rate to lend it out at a higher interest rate to make more money was not just how Liberty made money but any lending institutions; this is banking 101, whether its mortgages or even say personal loans, take deposits in and lend them out in the form of personal or auto loans at a higher interest rate. It was very sales-y, as competition was always fierce and customers could shop around, there were a lot of options in the region that you were competing against, a call for an inquiry to see what we were offering to ten different places and you would just hope you would get a chance to represent them. I think, at first, when I wouldn't close a deal, I would get mad, I felt like I had the best product and presented myself well but over the course of time and really just taking a step back while I never told the boss this you are going to get rejected a lot of times in sales and you cannot take it personally, you just say, "Well, I hope they got a good deal," and move on with a positive attitude.

This took me quite a while to come to grips with and to this day, I am not really sure why. There were goals that were expected to be achieved which, I guess, was cause number one but I had service time with the bank and would hope that a few slow months I would be granted a little bit of slack after proving to be a dependable and professional asset. I also cared a lot, which seems really corny to say but listen, I am sure you have seen in it just name a workplace in any field, co-workers that just show and do the bare minimum collect the check and that's it and not put forth *any* extra effort for whatever reason, one will never know and I didn't want to be that person, that's not how I was wired and how I was taught growing up.

Chapter 5
Love Starts on a Saturday

The Saturday coverage schedule was a little frustrating because it changed all the friggin' time and sometimes on Friday at 4 p.m. when you are trying to set the weekend up. The second part of that unique scheduling set up is you were set to switch between two different locations, if you were not permanently stationed at one location every day, barring a real emergency and lack of coverage at another location. So, yeah, trying to get three different people with families, kids, social life outside of work to ensure a branch was staffed correctly was a fun puzzle.

This particular Saturday took me to the Liberty branch on Wolf Rd., a very busy double lane in both directions stretch of commercial businesses directly across from a recently renovated shopping center and lined with businesses ranging from mom and pop's shops to franchises and larger corporations. A very busy branch that usually required two desk staff on a given shift. Desk staff are considered non-tellers that help with any transactions not regarding deposits and withdrawals, which, even on a Saturday, there are usually at four tellers working to help meet the demand. This is a lot and it is necessary to handle the traffic flow in this location to serve customers. I never really covered this particular location but knew the business that this location offered but didn't really know much of the staff and the regular manager was off (obviously, that's why I was there).

It was a pretty smooth sailing shift. Saturdays were usually pretty casual with a different vibe, then the Monday-Friday grind. Customers were excited it was Saturday so their mood was usually better.

Dating life was pretty inconsistent, given how the year started, but spending a lot of time with family and friends that were headed to the family lifestyle road. I knew that's what I wanted also but you can't just snap your fingers and *poof*, be married with a house and a fenced-in yard with the dog running and kids playing on the swing set. Not being a regular staff member at the branch, I had no key or code to lock up at the end of the shift, which was 1 p.m., and the slow walk to the door usually starts a few minutes prior to ensure a quick exit for employees. She opened the door, exiting the teller line, and started toward the front door and where the desk I was stationed at, she would be walking ten feet in front of me. She offered a "having fun yet," to which I stumbled to reply and to this day, I am not even sure if I mumbled coherently, "Tons of if, nothing better on a Saturday."

Thinking to myself, *my lord, this woman is beautiful*, and then thought, *Fat chance*. There is zero chance, negative chance she is single, not that I would have just blurted out, "Hey, want to go out on a date?" while at work to a coworker, usually ill-advised but not something that was completely taboo.

My schedule went back to normal, covering my usual locations with a rare trip to a random destination, again, being a floater, that is going to happen, but they tried meaning the schedule gods to keep me in a reasonable distance to where I was living at the time so it wasn't that terrible but I started seeing other assistants that had been in the same role; start getting placed in slower locations usually indicating lesser traffic as "show me" chances, which were, "We are going to station you here, show us results and you could be looking at a branch manager position."

Teller, *check*, assistant manager, *check*, now the focus was branch manager, a very aggressive goal but one I felt I could achieve. We would check the schedule Thursday, Friday; sometimes, they were also late getting the next week's schedule out also, which was scramble mode to piece a schedule together but it happened, finally, it read *"Jim Marshall"* (always thought James was to formal and I wasn't that formal) Hill Road, Week, score, that means no branch to branch each day since there was no manager at this location for several weeks after the previous manager who I actually went through orientation with got promoted to a busy store. It was in a good location with few competitors directly nearby and far enough away from the nearest Liberty Branch, where you could draw your own customer base. Now this branch was tiny and I mean in terms of space inside the facility, there are hotel suites that have more space to roam around in. I didn't care. I finally hit the landing spot of the "show me" chance and not just a fill-in for the manager that was out.

Not kidding, the first Thursday I was there, who do I see approaching the front door, *her*, there was no communication after the one random Saturday shift a few months back, I really figured there wasn't any reason to try and pursue it. Meanwhile, I don't see her in the branch, where'd she go? A.T.M.

I jumped up like I just hit the booster button and headed to the vestibule between the branch and front door where the A.T.M. was located. This time I started us off, "Hey, how's it going? How have you been?" all the while she was just trying to take some cash out, which, by the way, never does this to a person at the A.T.M. because a lot of things could happen and this list of good ones is pretty short. I was feeling good, I was in one spot, she actually was working in a different location now and I went for it, "Hey, I'm going to be out tomorrow at the Collar City Tavern (Friday)," which was a bar located about three blocks away from where I was living with three other buddies. Hail Mary! Never usually a high percentage play option but to switch sports, you miss 100% of the shots you don't take. I heard a, "Yes," and it wasn't just me imitating how I imagined she would say yes. Samantha said yes, I didn't even know her last name yet. Real fancy I know a sports bar and screams *"class, class, class,"* but it's the company and conversation and not the price tag, well, that's what I was surely hoping for. Something worked because there was another date then another, we were clicking, yes, I found out her last name was Lindman and she was four years younger, sport's fan, grew up in the same area and had an older brother, and obviously was also in the banking field, so we had a lot of similarities as a good base. The first time I had dinner at her parents maybe when she finally confessed to them she was dating someone, I guess, her dad and brother's name is Stephen spelled that way, well, I guess, I just figured it was spelled how it sounds Steven and joked the only way to spell it right with the V, her dad kindly pointed out it was in fact the other way and insert foot to mouth but tried to salvage and make a great remark on how amazing her mom's cooking was and that I, in fact, just started to like to cook also but no way matched her level. You still never know how or if you will even connect with someone but we did, I guess timing was just right but we hit it off and even started living together after a year of dating. Sam was a rockstar and way outta my league, there's a clever saying related to football when one team needs to kick the ball to the other team after a score or punting the ball after a failed series and it goes "outkick the coverage." This relates to dating when you would typically think that one person in a said relationship was better looking or maybe had money and the other party didn't, you get the picture, in my case, it was surely looks because Sam was gorgeous, but timing was right for both of us, I guess, and it just clicked for the two of us. Blond hair, blue eyes, looked absolutely stunning in a dress when we had to get fancy, even helped smooth over the fact that, meh, she came from a Yankee loving family I could deal with, most of my family actually rooted for the Yanks also but my dad was a Met fan so that's where I aligned. She was funny, quick witted, and kept me on my toes. Down to earth and not high maintenance and enjoyed our pizza wing and beer dates just as much as getting balled up for a wedding of a friend or family member. She got along and clicked really well with my family, which was a testament to her personality, and I would like to think that I clicked with her family pretty well also but at the end of the day, we were on cloud nine all the time.

We were having fun, traveling, going out anywhere and everywhere, baseball games, it makes for fun bantering each Subway Series, me being a Mets fan. Cruises, all inclusive, in the Bahamas and long weekend trips up to camp when it wasn't being used. I guess, sometimes, you can go the opposite way. I would have had zero issue getting married sooner but we were having a blast, were both secure in our jobs and enjoyed the time, which is all that life comes down to. I think we both knew that we would get married and it didn't even need to really be communicated. After two years, we had a long weekend trip to Florida planned to get some end of summer heat and sunshine and I decided this was the time after dating for over two years, I wanted to make Sam my wife. I had this elaborate plan all set to go, I would propose on the balcony of the suite we would be staying in during our trip the first night we were there and kind of turn the rest of the trip into a mini celebration. Didn't happen, I was so excited and I already received her parent's blessing after asking them (kind of an older tradition but I still felt it meant something to do this). I agreed with the jeweler to pick it up on Friday because we were leaving the next day and I didn't want it in the house we were renting in time more than a few days. I also started wondering how I was secretly going to pack it and go through security at the airport, so I decided that the Florida plan was scrapped and I was doing it when I got home, and we could use the Florida mini-vacation to celebrate. I got out of work slightly later than her and just told her I had to fuel up some gas before getting home. This was when I took the quick detour to the jeweler, picked up the ring, and ventured down the hill to our house. She was sitting in a chair, watching TV, ready to go out for dinner and I got down on one knee and asked her to marry me.

We had a pretty corny running joke with family and friends who were curious when we were gonna tie the knot, again, we were enjoying the moment, having tons of fun, and it just wasn't a priority at that moment, so we would always joke that the date had been set for summer of 2027, some sixteen years down the road from the present time. That was us, funny, corny, enjoying every minute of our time together.

Chapter 6
Marriage Bliss

We were usually always in the honeymoon phase anyways, so it was going to be interesting to see how life would be like after you know the actual honeymoon. Wedding was a complete party in June 2011 with family and friends dancing the night away and Zach smooth-talking the hotel concierge to let the wedding party into the swimming pool hot tub way after closing hours and after post-reception, beverages at a nearby Buffalo Wild Wings. The actual honeymoon took us to the Island of St. Lucia for a week long, all-inclusive beach paradise vacation. Although I missed the travel agent's heads up that the restaurants were business casual, meaning pants and a polo short, not sandals and shorts, whoops, a visit to the resorts gift shop for a nice pair of slacks was completed on day one. Frozen mixed drinks by the pool by day, dinner at night at the beautiful seaside restaurant, and no need to turn on the TV that was in the room, we just used the different spaces in the room for hotter than the island sun sex.

Back to real life, after the wedding and honeymoon, everything felt pretty much the same but did we want to expand the family with some kiddies, just like getting married, we were enjoying traveling and the freedom to be able to go out and socialize whenever we wanted at the drop of the hat. What we were able to accomplish, however, was the purchase of a home on the east side of Troy in a quiet neighborhood and a place to call our own. I think even before we were set with a closing date, Sam started looking at adoption sites and animal rescues for a dog. Her family always had one and the current family dog, Bailey, a beautiful German Shepard, needed a new friend. We found someone that had Labrador puppies ready for claiming so we took the drive out to Ravena to have a peak. We fell in love and placed our deposit request in but it came with a small caveat, we had a trip set to Baltimore to watch the Orioles and Yankees, Baltimore is a tremendous baseball city and awesome environment around the inner harbor, which we would have picked up the last pup without being able to pick, the breeder agreed that was fine since it was only going to be a few extra days.

The Yankees at the time had a fun-loving player named Nick Swisher, hmm, I'd had never met a dog named Swisher; had the nickname already of Swish set to go, and yes, I am well aware we named him after a Yankee I lobbied for Eli, pretty strong (New York Giants Super Bowl winning Q.B.) to no avail. I was already working well at the marriage compromise scheme. If you are keeping tally at home, marriage, house, dog all within the span of four months, we were really excited. I worked my way into a mid-level Liberty Branch, doing well and enjoying the banking industry learning and developing constantly and always trying to get better and Sam was in a great location with a different bank now Collar City Savings Bank, a relatively smaller institution with several locations within the capital district. Being able to get a dog-sitter for us to still be able to travel proved to be easier than discussing who would potentially watch kids for a whole week so we could go away.

We had plans to have children at some point in the future. We thought we would both be good parents and growing the family with little ones was both a tremendous thought but at the same time, also terrifying. Well, the time came upon us, two years after getting married and a few more vacations, Sam woke me one morning at 5:30 a.m., I don't know I think she read or heard it somewhere that taking a pregnancy test first thing in the a.m. produced a better pee test. Who knows and who am I to argue? Test in hand, "I'm pregnant."

I couldn't be more excited for us; Sam was going to be a rockstar of a mamma and I would just ride her coattails of love and compassion. Gut feeling, right off the rip, we started guessing boy or girl. We hadn't even been to the doctor yet for an official test and had to keep mum to family for a few weeks. I was convinced we would have a girl, I guess, part because that's what I actually thought and a little bit of reverse psychology mixed in, you know, maybe guess one way hoping for the other. Either way, I was pumped and would be praying for Sam to be safe during the pregnancy and for a healthy baby. Twenty week check up with the OB/GYN in for an ultrasound, Sam on the table, getting gooped up, and monitors all hooked up to tell us the sex of the little bundle of joy.

We were doing pretty solid with potential boy's names, quickly listing off several strong suitors with middle names pretty quickly. We wanted to find out the sex and planned on telling family the sex as well; girl's names, on the other hand, wowzas, stump city, even with google searches. Baby name books, the girl's name list was maybe three names and even then it became, "Well, let's wait for the gender and we'll come up with one by birth."

I knew what the ultrasound technician was going to say, I knew what I was going to hear, Sam asked how I knew so confidently and I guess I really didn't have a good answer for that question but I knew.

"Congratulations! You are having a baby girl"

Now I am not a rocket scientist, so saying, "I told you so," never crossed my mind but quickly turned my attention toward Sam and I knew it!

Sure, you dream of the sport days with your son, I was blessed with my dad and grandfather always being active in my sports days and I looked forward to hopefully being able to enjoy the same type of relationship if I had a son. Honestly though, think of the daddy/daughter bond and guess what girls can play sports, too, and have made great strides in availability and acceptance for women in sports even just through the last decade. We painted the room flamingo pink, what a name, but it was beautiful, watching Sam buy little dresses and matching shoes, going out shopping with her mom to buy essentials, really enjoying the moment. Sam was blessed with a healthy pregnancy, even beating the summer heat, thank goodness for swimming pools and central air conditioning and delivering our beautiful healthy daughter at Bellevue Women via cesarean section on a beautiful upstate New York morning in September (September 22nd, to be exact) 2013. Paige

Elizabeth Marshall ringing in at eight lbs. seven ozs., momma and baby completely healthy. We were in love; we knew we wanted to start a family and it was a job we were ready for but we didn't know that it was the job we needed. Complete love and admiration and excitement for the road ahead.

Paige enjoyed sleeping, ate pretty well, and whenever we ventured out to family gatherings or treated ourselves out, people were stunned at how relaxed and calm of a baby she was. I like to think that's because she knew how awesome her parents were but we struck the magical baby gold. We were now asked, since this baby was so chill, it was when we would move on to number two. We would always look at each other and smile, and give a half-hearted chuckle. Sam wanted a little boy also but when meeting Paige, we realized we were gonna be fine either way and wanted to enjoy this blessing while we could. I think we both wanted more than one kid but since this was our first rodeo, we didn't know what to expect and didn't want to rush to number two right away, some people do, to each their own, we wanted to enjoy this little darling. We eventually landed on the same page about having another one but let's wait a few years before bringing in another child into the mix.

Being able to venture to the camp with Sam and Paige for a week-long trip or a random day was pure joy. Feeling the drool spot on my shirt after a long day of playing at the beach and in the camp. It was now transferred to my brother and myself after the passing of Dad and Pappa, the younger Marshalls to take over primary care of the property and taxes and maintenance of the camp, as well as the dole out to the family for stays and when and how many weeks we would rent it out. It was great to keep this gem in the family, even facing the possibility of being able to fetch a haul back to spread out through the family. Party of five would soon be making frequent trips to the camp, that's right, Sam and I welcomed a baby boy into the world April 16th, 2015, Landon James Marshall (L.J.) to round out the family, two awesome kids and a doggo living the good family life. We upgraded to a nice 2016 silver Chevy Tahoe, Sam refused to drive a minivan, didn't like the look of 'em. I had nothing against them. We always had them growing up, helped for the family trips and with all the sports gear to fit whatever season it was. Anyhow, no bigs, the larger vehicle helped with the storage to head to the camp in one trip. Being able to venture to the camp now with my own family and when we would be up there with family, I see why my family enjoyed it so much and treasured it so much.

Chapter 7
Surprise Party

Having a late July birthday, the twenty-fourth of the month Sam was usually guaranteed a bash at the camp depending on the day of the week it fell on and if we were blown away with a rental offer that we could not refuse but this next birthday was off the books, her thirtieth birthday fell on a Saturday! The perfect opportunity for me to finally throw her an epic bash with family and friends, she always took care of me and threw me a pretty great party that year at a brewery in Troy with unlimited chicken wings and locally brewed beverages. She was now staying home with Paige and L.J. due to no immediate daycare availability and well, our unwillingness to pay twelve hundred dollars a month to send them to daycare. Before she entered the banking field, she also had hopes of breaking through in the education field either as an elementary school teacher or daycare provider, man, am I glad that she found the banking road because I hate to play the what if game but that would have been a huge what if had she ended up in education.

How would I secretly get that many cars to the camp without her obviously suspecting something and there certainly would have been the tip-off, considering the camp's driveway held about six cars and the dirt roads were barely two car wide, so I had to tell everyone to park outside of the Pillars, the entrance to the little camp village. Now, there a couple of easy outs here, from time to time, especially, on Saturdays from 11 to one, there would be a town flea market held on the piece of land just next to the dirt driveway to head through the pillars. Another option was that, again, especially, in the summer, the Chestertown Charter would sponsor a 5K road race around the lake and that the same grounds were also a pretty popular spot to park. I opted for the 5K because the flea market would have required tents and an expectation of seeing you know actual people. The start of the 5K began just after the pillars so by the time I had planned to get to the camp, this would have been perfect. Yes, I made sure both were actually not happening that particular day. The actual camp, while we tried not to make a habit, could hold a lot of people between driveway space, which I made sure only us would be parked in a decent size garage; the inside of the camp and the deck and fire pit area would accommodate a good crowd for such a special party. I stressed to everyone to be at the camp at exactly 12:30 p.m. and we would arrive shortly after 1 p.m. which you always need to provide enough time for tardy people to get to the party no matter how many times the invite says "surprise" on it, people still wait until the last minute, quite impressive actually. She quickly noticed the cars and didn't see any typical signs for the flea market so she quickly asked if there was a 5K that day and I informed her that the usual July 4th day race was postponed since there was a bad thunderstorm that morning and they didn't want to take any chances. I drove 45, once making the turn through the pillars, so she wouldn't notice any cars or that's what I hoped, she yelled at me lol, "Slow down."

I apologized and told her my foot slipped and didn't transition to the brake quick enough. I instructed Zach to lead everybody out to the back of the camp which would have hidden people much better, this worked to perfection because her first sight of someone was not until we hit the sliding glass door leading out to the deck.

"Surprise."

Sam wasn't necessarily a fan of surprise parties but it was surely worth it and it even worked! Paige started school and was growing into her own little woman, L.J. was chasing Swish's tail, trying to grab it through the camp, and this was going to be a perfect day. I sent out actual invites through the mail, not just a Facebook invite, which probably would have gotten people to respond a little easier but I digress, Sam deserved it, friends, family, her parents who had now stayed at the camp with us several times, aunts, uncles, cousins, we hit fifty people!

Now obviously parties of this size were usually frowned upon by the locals as they did not want the camp village to be like Las Vegas and New York City, a village that never sleeps but this was a monumental occasion. I went through the proper channels and let the neighbors know with a polite email that it was Sam's birthday if they were going to be there, swing by, or if they could please kindly let their renters know. It was a Saturday night so not like it was a random Tuesday which would usually be cause for a little bit more rowdiness anyhow but we at least covered our behinds. I informed guests of two local motels if they wanted to crash instead of driving back home. The camp couldn't sleep everyone anyways so it's not like everyone was going to be staying over.

I loved grilling, that was the cooking Sam allowed me to do but I didn't want to be stationed at the grill for hours while trying to enjoy Sam on her special day, so I reached out to the owners of the Laketime Restaurant, they had recently started a catering service specializing in bringing the BBQ to your party so you wouldn't have to watch your whole party standing over the grill. We did ribs and burgers and dogs, the keg was cold and the cooler stocked with her favorite beer, Corona, and the limes ready to be dunked in. I wasn't exactly sure what her actual gift would be. I mean I threw her this badass party and we had started gearing away from the big gifts with the kids getting all the cool toys but we would still get each other something at least. One thing we always did when we went to camping was bake, cookies, bread, cakes, you name it, led by, of course, the chef in the house, Sam, and I remember running into the person who we still get our firewood from each visit and, now we order from the son but on one of his last visits, he mentioned that he had learned the crafting trade from his dad and was selling some items he pre-made or could take customized orders. We always forgot a rolling pin and usually required a trip to the store because we would always take it home with us for some reason instead of just leaving it at the camp, the light bulb went off, asked him to make a hand-crafted rolling pin, and on one handle, it would read "Master Chef Sam" and the other handle would read "We love you always" and as the handle spun all of our initials were engraved, yup, even "Swishy Man." We both had happy tears in our eyes when I gave it to her because while not diamonds or a bottomless bag of cash, we were in a great place; enjoying each other and the completeness of our family. It was a beautifully clear night that set up perfect for a fire to be enjoyed by the people that were staying the night at the local motel, which was far less than the amount of people that were there during the daytime hours so we were set.

Chapter 8
Crash

A great stay completed at camp for the week with the typical drive home on a Sunday morning fairly early to get home and settle back into "city life" or really back to reality and back to work life would be a better description. It was a pretty quiet October morning in Upstate N.Y., we usually got pretty lucky in October weather-wise, winter was on the horizon but the days were still relatively warm and the foliage up north was nothing short of breathtaking this time of year to walk around the little camp village surrounding the lake with the kids and breathe in the fresh air.

I would typically drive, barring the rare occasion I needed to send some weekly plans to my regional manager on what the sales plans would be for the week and any meetings I may have to set up and I liked driving the SUV and letting Sam just relax in the passenger side sometimes, as long as we did our part and tuckered the kiddos out during the camp visit her only chance to maybe catch a few quick *zzz*'s or enjoy the scenery heading south down the Northway. Traffic in this time of year was usually pretty light, nothing like the Sunday traffic during the summer bustle with Lake George and the horse track in Saratoga being open and generally, just more people visiting but that usually tallied off after Labor Day and made for October Sunday drives quite peaceful. We were traveling at a good speed, not race car speed. I always used the cruise control and would set it nine miles over the speed limit. In this case seventy four for a speed limit of sixty-five traveling in the right hand lane. The scenery on both sides was in full fall foliage effect. When out of the corner of my right eye, glancing over to the passenger side of the road toward the woods, I see this animal dart out from the woods, deer, this time of year was definitely deer season, trying to get food for the winter or running from being hunted either or you needed to be on high alert from both sides of the road but they are extremely quick and sometimes dart right out into the road; sometimes, they make it to the guardrail and stop. This one didn't stop, hop right over the guardrail right onto the shoulder and started to dart into the road, a quick jerk of the steering wheel left is about the last clear thing I remember, the rest is a bad dream, car switching lanes on all sides, rolling over from the stretch of highway between exits seventeen and sixteen to barely being able to open my eyes, seeing flashing lights and someone trying to get my attention to get a feel of the situation.

The car rolled several times and ended up in the median between north and south traveling traffic and the road was dipped slightly and wooded and travelled from what accident reconstruction exams showed was almost a quarter mile from initial serve from trying to avoid the deer. I was taken to Saratoga Hospital with a broken arm, bruised ribs, but nothing severely punctured, and not conscious at the time. Waking up was the true nightmare, I had my mom and brother, who rushed to the hospital right away to check on us, my first reaction was where Sam and the kids were. I needed to see them, they tried to calm me down with a nurse and a doctor in the room delivered the worse news that I had ever been given. The blunt force trauma during the rolling of the vehicle caused too many internal injuries for them to overcome. I almost went back unconscious and even prayed that this was a mistake or that I could have been the one not waking up, could not be happening not now. I should have just plowed through the deer and taken the damage to the right side of the vehicle to a body shop the next Monday. Then guilt sets in, this was all my fault and why did I survive? Take me, not them. Grief and sadness were back after I finally started to turn around after 2008 and battling depression. How do you think burying your soulmate along with two little innocent bright future children was going to trigger me now?

Cremated, even at our young age, we did, in fact, talk about wanting to be buried or cremated, so they were cremated together to be together and hopefully look down on me and forgive me. I was in the hospital for a week for monitoring mentally and physically and probably could have left a day or so sooner but I refused to eat, so they wouldn't discharge me until I ate some of the delicious microwaved chicken and instant mashed potatoes but the red Jell-O was made with love. A service for memory of life was held at Connor and McGoughlin Funeral Home in Troy on a rainy, dreary Tuesday. It was non-stop crying, disbelief, not even the flask hidden in my suit jacket filled with Jack took the edge off but I kind of expected it. Everyone was in disbelief. I took extended time allowed by

Liberty to evaluate next steps if returning to work at some point was even an option, they were great and told me to take care of me first and there would be no time limit on returning and that a spot would definitely be kept open for me to return in a manager role. I felt that was at least a nice gesture. I still had Swish to console me, although he kept looking for Mamma and the kiddos. Sometimes we would take him with us and he would be stationed between the kid's car seats in the back. This trip, however, he stayed at the in-laws to just get some other doggy playtime. I isolated with the dog; didn't venture out much, if at all, besides getting the essentials to maybe eat a meal and take care of the now empty house which was more depressing. We created such a beautiful home and now I didn't even sleep in our bedroom but shacked up on the couch with the TV on and the dog lying on the floor. It didn't help that I didn't really expect it to. Family and friends were great checking in on me, dropping some meals off, though they just went to the freezer. I lost ten pounds in three weeks because unlike at the hospital where they could threaten not letting you leave, all I had to do at home was, "Oh, yeah, I'm eating good."

Swish man was definitely taken care of, he may have found some of the weight I lost with the home-cooked delivery meals, we would try and go out in the yard get some fresh air and I would throw him the Frisbee but even that was a trigger of sadness, seeing the empty swing set in the corner of the yard, picturing Sam pushing Paige on the swing and Swish running around with excitement and L.J. just chilling in a nice shady spot.

What was I going to do next? Go back to work? The thought of that almost made me sick to my stomach as I went back sitting at my desk, trying to call potential customers and put on a happy smiley face, it was barely happening for friends and family, so why would I expect to be able to do it for strangers? I decided I was going to head to the camp for the winter with Swish and stay there. Zach agreed to watch the house, and stay there if the need called for it, take care of snow removal and check the water, keep the heat on low so the pipes wouldn't freeze. We would stash clothes at the camp, sometimes as extra storage so my packing wasn't overly complicated, stopping at the hardware store for a bulk purchase of pellets for the pellet stove was an essential pickup but I needed the isolation, trying to get day to day real life swirling around while you're in the epicenter of it not knowing what the next step will bring. The winter was always slower for renting purposes and family trips anyways. People preferred warm weather, beach time, and campfires at night. Growing up in New York and living through the winters, I enjoyed the snow falling and how nice it looked covering the trees so I welcomed the isolation that I would be providing myself. Not many neighbor camps were occupied during the winter either, so I wouldn't have to worry about neighbor traffic. I stocked up on groceries at the wholesale club store before packing the truck up and heading north. The grand union had long closed but a Stop N Shop took its place, so when I needed something, I had somewhere to go. Cell coverage was sufficient and the world came a long way since just three channel viewing, the camp was now equipped with Wi-Fi and a 43-inch TV, so I could plug in when I needed to. We would usually try and stash some non-perishables at the camp each year; just to have in case of a surprise trip or in case we were going to escape there for a while.

Since the tiny mantle was already filled with pictures and urns of my dad and my grandfather, I created a makeshift memorial in the living room on top of a nice wooden bookshelf for them to watch over me and be at a peaceful place that they loved to frequent. You may say that it was too depressing of a vibe in the camp now but let's face it, this is where these people had some of their greatest memories and we developed some of our fondest family memories, plus, the camp was hardly being rented out anymore to anyone outside of the family, so when someone other than Zach or I would stay there, it was more than likely going to be someone that actually knew what happened and would not be overly concerned or bothered by the funeral home vibe but sadly, this was the amount of loss that the Marshall Camp endured over the last several years.

Chapter 9
New Residence

Two months after living at the camp, I realized that after all the loss and suffering that staying in Chestertown permanently was what I wanted to do for the future, so I started taking steps to make that happen. Since Zach had been watching the house and was renting at the time, we started discussing him purchasing the house in Troy for a family special and with savings, the sale to Zach, life insurance money, and some stocks that paid off from the early years and since there was no loan on the camp, I could find a part-time gig in Chestertown for twenty-thirty hours or so at a retail store such as the Stop N Shop or even Landy's a prominent expanding convenience store booming in the northeast. Sam and I, after having kids, were pretty savings heavy and obviously, vacations stopped other than heading to camp, especially after L.J. was born, so outstanding debt other than a few credit cards was pretty reasonable. Plus now we wouldn't have to pay someone for snow removal, cleaning, and general check-ins at the camp if Zach or I wouldn't be able to make it. I was able to handle simple repairs and this wasn't a town of nothing; it had resources available in the forms of handy people that could help in a pinch. There was already a snow-blower in the garage of the camp, so purchasing one was not necessary at the time and a lawnmower was not needed as it was a driveway to a garage surrounded by pine trees in the front and deck and beach in the back.

I was finished with banking, selling Rose or Joe who was on fixed social security payments month to month, withdrawing cash each month to pay basic bills to hit a sales goal and visiting every realtor's office in the area was getting a little tiresome. How about taking care of customers and not losing the bank any unnecessary money and I mean that as in fraudulent activity, such as bad checks or fake money plots. It was a great learning experience and I was proud of the work I was able to accomplish but the time was right for me to move on, so I informed Liberty that my extended leave would become a permanent one and thanked them for their understanding. The house transfer to Zach went smoothly and I was still going to be close to the family that remained in the area but renting the camp was finished and visits would be minimal to extended family, which I understood may have upset the applecart but frankly, didn't give a fuck. I was taking care of me and if someone wanted to visit for a weekend, I had no issue accommodating a short stay; plus, the company and getting the part-time job would help keep my sanity and social skills at a functioning level. Plus, I still had Swish as my companion, man's best friend, can't get lonely when there's a fun-loving lab ready to hit the trails and jump off the dock chasing a tennis ball.

The one thing I was going to need major work on was cooking. Sam was the chef in our household, always preparing delicious home-cooked meals that she learned to make from her mom and grandmother. I could turn the stove on for her and I was a great taste tester before the food was plated to which usually led to a, "Hey, hey, hey, wait your turn like everyone else," and I would just reassure her that I had to make sure it was okay for the kids to eat before putting it on a plate, it was always O.K. and she would just give me the look of "you are full of B.S."

I truly missed her and the kids and at otherwise simple tasks like cooking or hearing a child laugh at the store or on the beach brought back so much pain and agony. The two camps near us once their original owners started getting older and passed just like my grandparents had, took advantage of the seller's market for such property and sold the camps and I get it, Zach and I thought about doing the same thing after Sam and the kids passed but decided not to make any rash decisions and held on to it. The thought of taking down the homemade Marshall sign near the front door was unfathomable to us.

I stayed away from the public beaches in the summertime. There was no real need for me to frequent them, other passing by on a walk through the makeshift dirt roads through the tiny little "camp village," which we came to call it, sitting out on the deck was nice and shady and provided a good view of the passing motorboats with tubers and skiers; plus, I had a dock to jump off to take a swim if the summer heat became too much. I would entertain in the summertime family that wanted to visit for the weekend. Zack would usually only be the lone winter visitor, he liked snowboarding, so this put him at a short drive to Gore Mountain and if he wanted to take a trip to Lake Placid and visit Whiteface Mountain, he could do so. I never really hit the mountains at all but had a pair of snowshoes and cross-country skis ready to go in the garage of the camp to keep my exercise levels up during the winter. Grocery trips were few and far between because long gone were the $300.00 shopping trips; although, I would always love putting the groceries away to see what snacks I was going to eat first and drool at what Sam would be cooking up for the next few weeks. Sometimes, when I would check up and see the total of $100, I would tear up a little and be on my way back to the camp. My grandmother had a cookbook at camp and Sam had a cookbook passed down to her that I was allowed to keep and brought with me to the camp, plus, an endless opportunity for YouTube videos and *Food Network* competitions and restaurant saving shows. I would be the next Gordon Ramsay before you knew it.

The seasons turned and the lake stayed peaceful and I was settling into a permanent resident of the North Country; even growing my lumberjack beard out, which was always frowned upon on the business suit requirement of the bank and the clean-cut Yankee style that was expected. I landed an opener position at Landy's for thirty hours a week just off the exit you would take to head toward the lake. Serving coffee to log truckers in the a.m., welcoming incoming guests as they pit stop after however long they were on the road for and goodbye-ing people that were just visiting or people that were summer residents; it kept the social interaction up and enough to where I was not a TV dependent talking to your dog only introvert. Although a piece of my socialization died after the accident, I felt invincible with Sam at my back and that I could accomplish anything and would be able to close a deal with any business prospect or potential lending client. That desire and confidence stayed in the Chevy Tahoe on that drive back after our last stay at the camp.

There were actually a few psychologists in town that I had bounced around to see which one I would like potentially longer treatment with. The grief and depression, along with the new lifestyle were changing and past events that going to go speak with someone was something that I probably put off after the loss of Dad, Pappa, and Kevin but now also getting older and having to travel back to the Capital Region for more funeral services of friends and family members was getting to be a lot but I leaned on Zach who, pretty much like me, suffered loss from Dad and Pappa and we needed to be there for each other whenever we needed it. Campfires in the summertime with a glass of whiskey, hashing up old memories of previous camp trips in the burning flames, hearing faint laughs from other fire pits in the distance, long gone were the days of booming parties at the Marshall Camp and that was okay, they served as great memories, even if the main dish was seasoned with sadness and despair. The tiny little village that had pretty good spacing between each camp now, so some owners selling off parts of their land too eager to pay and build out-of-towners looking for a summer escape. The bustling city life for "Lake Time" Development was everywhere, some lavish depending on the size of the land available and some just enough space to fit in between two camps but not in my particular area, the land was kept, though the people that purchased and obviously Zach and I were certainly not interested in selling any of our land off.

Chapter 10
Solitary

Walking with a now grey bearded Swish throughout the grounds and touring what new properties were sandwiched in and what new spaces were created and wondered who moved into where and how much fun their families were having or if they rented it out for the week to a family that had never been here before did they feel like this could become a new family tradition vacation spot. That feeling had long gone for me and now it was the crackling of pine cones in the fire or the peacefulness of the lake in the morning that I sought out and brought me some resemblances of normalcy. The ice cubes hitting the bottom of the whiskey glass before the Jack goes in and the birds chirping in the tree. Long gone was my desire to host any family parties and cater to people that wanted to use the camp, even if it was just for a weekend. I mean it was completely social isolation; there were friendly hellos at the grocery and liquor stores and the half-hearted wave when I would walk the trails during the summer. Zach would come up and stay for a weekend here or there and the camps around us were still there and would have families visit from time to time, so a wave and hello were always in order.

I would often ponder at the camp that originated the story from my dad and grandfather and thought maybe the boy was on to something, not that he really had a choice but what choice did I have? Just like him losing his parents at a young age, there were losses on my side that were just as heartbreaking and why not seek refuge away from irritating bosses, noisy cars, and city life; not that the Capital Region was anything close to what being near New York City was like, it still was a very different lifestyle than living on the lake and some days, I would wonder if I made the right choice to move away and isolate but that was better in my opinion than stay home and try and pretend like everything was normal and go about daily life as if nothing ever happened and it was all smiles and rainbows still. The lake offered a fresh start and I could take my grief with me and learn how to cope and deal and try to live a life that many wouldn't want or even understand but how many people would have been able to understand the loss and grief that had seemed to make a normal appearance in my life? Depending on people's personalities and lifestyle choices, this was not going to be for them and that's fine, I get it, and I wasn't going to sell them on why I thought it was best for me, that's all that matters was that this was best for me and really, once I moved passed, trying to defend it, which was really silly of me to try and do, I didn't have to sell myself on it.

The calmness of the lake first thing in the morning while the steam from my coffee rises with the fog off of the lake, walks and runs around the lake, boats zooming around eating breakfast and dinner with Swish on the deck; remember, I was not the cook, so cooking two meals a day now for me was a great accomplishment; plus, wanted to stay a little trim and take care of myself was something that Sam would always bark at me for with good reason, it was always a sprint to the goodie cabinet to see what the grocery produced in regards to snacks. Plus, Swisher getting older, reaching an age where I needed to watch his consumption and keep his activity level up was just not as important but actually more important. I got pretty good practice because one night of cooking a plate of chicken and rice for the Swish man, that little fucker stopped eating his dry food, so I would now be cooking for two each meal, the dinner conversation was at least interesting, we would talk sports, "Did the Mets win that day? Did the Giants blow a game on Sunday or whenever they were playing N.F.L. games at that particular time?"

I found myself rekindling old lake hobbies, such as doing puzzles and playing solitaire, Zach and I would play a game of *WAR* from time to time to provide us with a few chuckles from memories of simpler times playing a simpler card game for two simple brothers. Even looking into the burning fire at night seemed to be more peaceful in the summertime.

Winters saw a little more snow being slightly farther north than Albany but having the snowblower oiled and gas ready-made it for a breath of fresh air to clear the driveway when needed and to get Swish out of the camp as well. The town would clear a path usually the following day to provide at least a single car lane for visitors or residents to travel safely through. Having never really liked it or loved shoveling snow before even this became a sense of appreciation at the beauty of the snowflakes falling into the

71

lake and then the majestic view of the snow-covered pines surrounding the lake, who would have thought even that I actually started using the cross-country skis throughout the trails during the wintertime for some added exercise and view of the now winter covered campgrounds. I would keep a nice slow pace depending on where we were and how much snow we had to allow Swish to keep pace. Most of the time, I would just try to keep on the snow plowed path to make it a little easier on him. Zach's winter visits became more sparse as he was getting ready to settle down with his now fiancée and starting the journey of starting a family in the house in Troy just like Sam and I once had. The grocery trips were less crowded and the liquor store was not as bought out so I would usually take this time to stock up on my two new friends, Jack and Jim, and the essentials at the grocery store that would usually go a little quicker in the summertime like toilet paper, cleaning supplies, and paper towels. Camps needed to be cleaned in between visits of renting customers for obvious reasons, so these items became in hot demand toward the end of May as schools started letting out around a month later. Depending on how the winter was going, coldness wise in January and February would usually see the coldest of temperatures which would make the lake freeze. I was not a fishing person but I would step off the dock from time to time and see if it was time for a brief venture onto the lake for a short distance. The view in the wintertime on the lake itself was magical, snow-covered trees and beaches smoke from the fireplaces or wood stoves from the camps that were actually inhabited during the time, sometimes just bringing a chair onto the ice and sitting there, taking it all in was just as peaceful as watching the water move at night during the summertime. Work hours were reduced because there just wasn't as much traffic so the stores sales slowed down, so I would have more time off for reading and exploring and hanging out with the Swish man, which was fine because I would always bank the end of summer checks and winter furlong payments and use my weekly shift money for essentials, so there was still cash flow and enough to pay the necessities like Wi-Fi and the electric bill.

I wasn't too interested in getting back in the dating scene which had more opportunities during the summer time with more visitors whether local or from out of town which sure may have led to a few one-night affairs but any interest past that I was not interested in ever again. I had the best family life already and the thought of potentially trying to embrace that and enjoy that feeling again was not something even over the course of a few years passing since the accident and my still relatively young age, my one shot was Sam and the memories of the family life we enjoyed was not going to be replicated by anyone and I was not going to invest any effort into entertaining the idea of giving it a second chance. To me, that would have defeated the purpose of having the camp become my primary residence, if love was something I wanted again, I would have just stayed in Troy and went about the same every day back and forth to work and maybe have a friend of a friend be available or someone I met through work or at a social gathering and even dating apps, hundreds of dating apps that were available, I probably could have even joined one up in the north country AdirondackLove.Com or I imagined something along those lines on where I could go. Sam was it for me, no matter how Zach thought, it was time to move on just because he was starting his family. I thanked him for his concern but assured him I was going to be okay.

Have you sat out in the middle of a lake on a boat and idled the motor or kayek'd and just put the paddle to rest and watched a sunset? Any body of water for that matter and just watch the sun sink into the tall pine trees, the water sports are completed for the day as everyone is tired out from a day on the water and settling down for dinner but bringing a flask out in the middle of the lake to enjoy the peace and serenity seeing all the nightly fires started to reach their apex when it gets dark to enjoy the summer nights and unwind from a great day around the fire and think life was going pretty good. I was settling in just fine over the course of a couple of seasonal cycles. In the sunset moments or winter views of the lake, I often wondered where Sam and I would be at this particular point in our lives, bigger house, another dog, another kid? The great what if during the gaze to the stars and slow tears running down my cheek about the kids and how we would have watched them grow up and what they would have been doing at this exact moment. This never really helped and what-if-ing it was surely not helping anything, the loss was great and least I could try and do was enjoy the moments and take joy in the life we were able to have for, even just a brief time and try and come to inner peace that accidents will happen all over the world where people will lose their livelihoods in the blink of an eye or in our case, a dart of a scared deer jetting into the road. These were not the exact memories that I was looking to extract when doing these activities but sometimes seeing the beauty of God's land but then asking while looking up at the sky, why, in that exact moment, was it time for my wife and kids to be taken from me? Before it became our camp, my grandmother had a Bible in the drawer in the master bedroom that she would read some verses to us from time to time, maybe she thought we needed it, but I would often open the top drawer and glance at that same Bible that was still there but that's usually where that would end in just reading the title, and never really made it out of the drawer.

Chapter 11
2023

Swish and I didn't really watch the news; we could pretty much sum it up between us now, him the seasoned sports broadcaster and doubled as the weatherman, me as the lead anchor of course and field reporter would jokingly do a broadcast back and forth, "And now over to Swish for the daily sports recap."

"Ah thanks, Jim, had some great action in the N.B.A, last night and even the Knicks got a victory."

Other anchors laughing.

"Onto weather it's going to be a nice stretch of springtime weather ahead for the next seven days so make sure if you have fur friends, get them outside after a long winter of snow and cold."

Of course the Swish man would throw that in there but now him and I competing for the camp's Mr. Greybeard a nice easy paced walk put him in his glory as I was unsure of how long labs were supposed to live for but this one is going to be the first one to live forever, fine, I knew that to be false and just hoped that the nature around the lake would help breath the fresh oxygen into his bloodstream maybe giving him a few extra years. With all the mobile and email alerts and even the rare occasion to pick up a newspaper in print, kind of a bunch of typed words on paper folded into different sections that were almost as extinct as the dinosaurs and texts from Zach from time to time, it wasn't that hard to stay in the loop as to major goings on in the area and the world.

I was still able to vote on all pertinent elections; local town board members, state senators, governor, president. So we would follow along and I would ask Swish for his breakdown on the candidates and which ones he thought were going to treat us the right way and be stand up people which would usually garner a pretty good chuckle because politicians and standup people were not usually synonymous with one another, but they all sure promised the world and how and what they were going to do and why they were *so* much better than the other person/persons they were running against. This was an off year for the biggie elections, president, governor, town board elections would be held in November but the next year was going to be the big election year, so, naturally, one year out you start seeing candidates jump in the pool and start making their case, why they would be great for New York or even the United States, so we would take note of the names would see how the political parties would align over the next twelve months during debates and advertising and open public forums for each to present their case. When Sam and I had Paige, we would often joke that we were changing the diaper of the first woman president, we both hoped that it surely would not take that long but knowing politics a little bit and starting to follow it that sadly who would have even known if by the time Paige was eligible that one would have been elected by then.

We had the camp protected in the version of a double barrel break action shotgun that was handed down from my grandfather who purchased for the sole purpose to keep at the camp for a few different reasons, there was always a possibility of a bear wandering to the camp or being that it was a decent tourist area during the summer, that vandalism could be an enticing way for a wanna-be criminal to try and make a good buck. We never hunted or anything like that and him and my dad would take Zach and I out to just really show us the basics and respect for the gun itself. We were instilled with respect for the gun and respect for using it in only emergency situations and how to clean and handle it. We would get a refresher every couple of summers or so, just to make sure we were still adapt in how to handle it, plus the same family that dropped our wood off would let us go into their back woods and fire several rounds at some barrels of hay or trees or whatever the makeshift target of the season was. It actually turned into a pretty good stress reliever once I moved there permanently to get Swish in the truck and swing by the woods again and fire off some rounds. Two g's now were my hobbies; gun and golf in the summer and cross-country skiing and sitting on the frozen lake in the winter time. The gun was now just under the bed at night but always growing up, it was locked in a case and I actually never really knew where it was until my grandpa and dad took Zach and me the first time to the field and saw it come out of the case.

An A.W.N. (America World Network) came across the phone; this was per the usual at least several times per day as the goings on nationally and sometimes even globally if it was something of note. *New virus hits Arica Chile,* so you can either click the link and read more about it or just disregard and move about whatever you were going to look into on your phone; for me, it was which sporting event was happening at that particular time because one thing that did not fade away was the love of sports and watching them so I was always checking scores and would usually have multiple devices running at any given time, TV, phone, computer, especially during football season because Swish and I were able to now bet legally without stepping foot in a casino, what a world, right? So, of course, we hit the pass button on that news alert and go about our daily lives.

The lake was still thriving and camps were bustling in the summertime and I would enjoy the private dock and boat space to cool off whenever needed in the summertime. The summer renter rate was still going to be pretty high according to the report that would be circulated throughout the lake residents, which usually provided how many renters had already booked so far potential opportunities for additional rentals to be listed and what the average price per week would be and would also show any properties being built or any properties that would be hitting the market for purchase, which was usually good to look at for property values and the rental rate was always beneficial since if it was a high summer of say 80% rented that would mean a high out-of-towner season but I would never fault the property owner for renting during peak season, doing this could help pay the bills for the property depending on when it was purchased, if a second mortgage was taken out on someone's primary residence or some other form of funding was used seeking to rent during the summertime was a great way to make some of these funds back and even profit. I still enjoyed numbers, sports numbers, money numbers, obviously percentages of renters, sales/listing prices of camps, I would always joke that I was never really good in math during my school years but I developed a great understanding and knowledge for real world math during my banking days and during Sam and my first few years of marriage and with young children, you learn real quick about what is going to get paid or what may be waiting a few weeks.

Around early March or so, I took the Swish man to the vet, he seemed like he had a pretty nasty stomach bug with vomiting and all that fun stuff but overall, he was still his normal self, goofy and hyper, they say pets take on the personality of their owner so what does that tell you about me. Doc looked him over and put him on some antibiotics and we went about our way. The pet doc was right in town and had seen Swish a few times and that's where we would get his tick prevention from spending a lot of times in the summer time was always a necessity to stay up to stay up to date with that medication and even with his age now, doc said he looked pretty darn good. Fast forward two months and Swish just wasn't right, eating less, while good, he was eating a little bit, limited movement, not his normal playful self, drinking water like he had just been told his water supply was going to be cut off in sixty minutes and he definitely lost weight, Swish was always extremely fit, never fat, eighty pounds of love and muscle. He was my companion now and was always my best friend although and I'll be completely honest, he was a mamma's boy! Man,

80

did he love Sam, I would be jealous but there was something so beautiful seeing the two of them together. After the accident, I knew he was a little off but we were always best friends and I adored him more than ever and needed this to just be another virus or he ate something that some antibiotics could kill.

Even though it was a fairly small doctor's office, they had the resources to do a lot of the work needed right there to give some definitive answers with x-rays and blood work but the prognosis was not good. Sadly, at this point, me expecting more would have been out of the question, having faced all the negative calls and realizations that maybe just this once I would not get a doom and gloom outlook. Please, God, at least once, literally throw me a bone so I can play fetch with Swish again, but why would this scenario be any different.

"Hi, Jim, unfortunately, after reviewing the results of the bloodwork and scans we took of Swish, this is not a viral or digestive issue that will be treated with antibiotics."

"Okay, fine, here's my credit card and I'll drop off cash."

I usually kept a secret stash under the mattress just in case and let's get this healed up.

"The cancer has spread quickly throughout his body and our main focus right now will be to keep him comfortable and we will need to discuss with you in the office about next steps."

I put the phone on speaker after cancer and grabbed the nearest chair. Why, after everything else, would this be any different? I mean I should have fucking expected it by now that this was exactly how it would happen.

The doc's office was great and very understanding and even gave me a little almost like a dog tag with his name and date lived and a circular piece of wood with a dog's paw print in it and Swisher engraved in it. I slinked back to camp, grabbed a pint glass, and filled three parts jack and a dash of coke, and sat on the deck and cried. Maybe some people don't have pets for one reason or the other, allergies, too much work, don't want them around the children, feel like it's too much of a burden, living arrangements, so be it, but Sam always had a dog growing up and although I had a few sporadically, never one for an extended period of time. This was going into summer when we would always have a blast, hikes, swimming, beers on the deck, car rides with the window down, and now I just looking back at all the memories again; just left with looking up at the sky, askin' questions to everyone to see how they are doing. When the doc returned his ashes, they went to the spot on the bookshelf, so he could be closer to his mama. I always joked with him about being a mama's boy. It was a very nice wood crafted box that had a picture slot in the front of it so I placed a nice picture in there of him enjoying a nice summer day out on the deck at one of his favorite places.

Chapter 12
Lonely Nights

I had just started getting used to the whole cooking thing, breakfast in the morning and dinner at night out on the deck, nothing ever fancy like eggs benedict or beef wellington or prime rib but fancy for us was some pancakes and a couple of steaks on the grill for dinner. The joy was stripped away and I didn't see any real reason to cook for myself at all, so I switched to an instant oatmeal breakfast which I guess my doctor was at least excited about to watch the cholesterol, instead of firing up some bacon, but at least after the bacon, we would head out for an early morning stroll. Dinner? Sometimes, I opted for just the liquid version of calories with my buddies, Jack or Jim, or some Adirondack lagers depending on the day. It doesn't say on the can of Spaghettios that you can't be over the age of twelve and still be enjoying them. Zach was enjoying life in Troy and was busy starting his own family with his wife and I was happy for him, I really was, but visits were reduced quite a bit to almost none at all and sure, we would still text but we were always a show our love type of family, hugs, I love you's, you name it, and how much of that do you actually feel from the three little dots that pop up in a text message or reading the sent from my iPhone message at the bottom of an email signature. I will shoulder some of the blame. My desire to stay connected disappeared when Swish died at the doctor's and I lost the last piece of my puzzle and was not trying to purposefully alienate anyone but I was all alone and the tidal wave hit me all at once. Grief and loss is a process and even comes with stages and each person deals with grief and loss at their own pace but thinking back, had I ever sought the proper attention way back in 2008 or even after Sam and the kids were gone? Or did I plow ahead and focus on the road ahead because I still had a puzzle piece left. The conversations were one-sided now at night, which from turning into the news from time to time. They actually switched to more of a solo anchor type of show, Swish would always joke with me that he would be able to do the show on his own no problem and would get better ratings and more money, I always told him I was the straw to stir the drink with the people and their eyes and ears were tuning in to listen to me.

I would take the same trails and still sit out on the end of the dock to catch a sunset or watch the lake once all the motorboats were finished for the day and walking by the beaches and seeing families enjoying the summer heat by cooling off in the lake would make me smile for an instance and then I would forge ahead and put my head down and pick up the pace on my run or brisk walk. Wintertime and snow blowing the driveway just like the main road got one path which we would always get in trouble by Dad or Grandpa if we tried to hurry the snow removal to get back to the TV quicker, but now I hardly went out when it snowed, liquor was always stocked as well as the spare fridge in the garage full of beer that never ran out and my cuisine was, well, I ate what some would call food for calories but I wasn't breaking out the cookbooks anymore and I would just snow myself in and enjoy the pellet stove. I would still shovel off the deck, just in case we got that mild January day where the sun would be shining and it would be a breath of fresh air to feel refreshed and excited to be heading into the warmer months while enjoying the pretty scenery. One chair by the fire pit with a double of whatever the drink of the night was and sometimes both arms of the chair had a double drink. I dubbed them my "buy one, get one" special nights at the Marshall Mountain Pub House and watching the fire light up and some nights, I didn't make it inside the camp. I crashed on a patio chair so I would smarten up and set out a drunk blanket before heading down to the fire pit depending on mood-o-meter, I now called it; was it a full despair night, slight despair did seeing a family during the daily walks bring back too much sadness, did I catch a glimpse at a Cardinal in a pine and smile and actually make it inside the camp to sleep in the bed that night. There were no more loud cheers, watching the fireworks explode over the lake from my dock or loud laughs coming from my campfire area, just the drunken stumbles of patio furniture and picking up in the morning time.

The surrounding camps turned more rental as the years passed and it was mostly out-of-towners staying a week to week during the summertime. Assholes turned it into a money grab and a place for profit and continued to breathe in the shit for air in whatever city they were from. The wintertime I wouldn't even have to take the gun to the wooded area that we were accustomed to. If I didn't see smoke rising above the trees for a few days, it was safe to shoot a few rounds at beer bottles by the trees or old patio cushions that I would use as makeshift targets. From time to time, I would take the nice handcrafted rolling pin that I got Sam for her birthday and I would use it as a baseball bat to relive my glory days of high school baseball with any shot glasses that I could find, "Now up to bat, the Great Whiskeino."

It sure as hell wasn't being used for its intended purpose anymore, so why not improvise? It was collecting dust along with the passed down family cookbooks. I sold my golf clubs to a renter who really just wanted them for a round but I didn't golf anymore but I just said I didn't need 'em back.

I was still working though and that was a blast, dragging myself outta bed to work a few shifts here and there and most morning shifts, I felt like spitting in the coffee and yelling over the intercom to the gas pumps to tell the families fueling up for the ride home or after a long drive from home to go fuck themselves.

"Hey there, pump number two, welcome to Landy's. Oh, yeah, by the way, go fuck yourself."

There are restaurants that make fun of patrons, so why wouldn't this be thought of any different? Ohhh, because little Johnny and Suzie never heard a cuss word, please, they probably knew more than their parents with god knows what they were watching on television or videogames and the shitty so-called music of the times but I just thought it and gave a great big smile each time thinking I had just said it but the usual, "Thank you and hope you have a great day," was the usual goodbye.

I would still challenge myself mentally and physically just not with puzzles and books anymore, my mental challenges would come in the form of spitting challenges, trying to land my dip spit in the Mason jar wherever I felt like would give me the greatest challenge. I know a terrible habit that started in my younger days and would occasionally throw one in when at the lake taking a hike or a canoe trip across the lake. Sam would actually threaten to hit me with the rolling pin if she caught me doing it while we were there but the usage dwindled down to almost never for the obvious reason. It was a bad habit and two because that hand crafted rolling pin was no joke and Sam was certainly not joking about hitting me with it. The snap of the can to pack it out on the deck at sunset became a nice relaxing evening ritual, which was funny, because I always chuckled at the people who needed a cigarette first thing in the morning with their coffee or after sex, and Holy Lord, Sam and I weren't smokers but there were nights that it was so good that we considered starting but that's all. It stayed and we would joke about it after and ask each other to, "Go get the Marb Lights," or, "Pass me a Marb Light," before enjoying the amazing feeling of being with each other in a perfect moment. Don't get me wrong, there were angry nights between us, too. It's bound to happen on the crazy rollercoaster of life with work and kids and we would retreat to a separate area of the house or I would take a drive to cool my head, but we never ever fought at camp except an occasional bicker about why we should have chicken for dinner instead of ribs or why there was so much mayonnaise in the macaroni salad but that was it. Some nights, I would even miss that sitting out on the deck spit cup on one side and beer or drink of the night on the other because we both knew at the end of the day, we had each other's backs through whatever life was going to throw at us and we were in it together and there was no one I wanted by my side going through it than her, so, yeah, I'm only human and sometimes a tear would roll down my face and land into the drink. Who was going to see me anyways, so I didn't care.

It was suggested that I maybe go talk to someone about all the grief and loss that occurred and really the strides and awareness in the mental health field even just over a span of twenty years in my lifetime was somewhat remarkable. Just thinking of my dad and grandpa's days it was tough guy mentality and it was bottle it up and not talk about it. I would be lying if certain days I didn't strongly consider it; looking back, it probably would have been very beneficial after the accident but at this point, the lake was my therapy, and spending time in the woods with the birds and the trees was calming enough. I figured circling the wagons back to all the tragic events would do more harm than good, so, yeah, I grabbed a couple of Dack Lager bottles and brewed a nice batch of Jim's feelings I.P.A. Even in the wonderful world of technology, you didn't even need to travel to particular offices. Some doctors would be able to hold a session right over a video feed used by a computer, laptop, or phone. Who would have thought it felt like *the Jetson's* cartoon was finally coming to reality and the flying cars would soon be next. I figured coping on my own was fine and didn't want any medication or judgment. I knew what I lost and it was never coming back and I still kept myself active with hiking, enjoying the lake, campfires, although by myself. If the depression started eating away at those activities and *they* started to become tasks instead of respites of the everyday, then I may have further considered it into a possibility instead of just a thought or a recommendation from Zach or someone else. I knew the alcohol or dip wouldn't help anything go away, I wasn't trying to run away from my feelings. I knew full well I was in a state of depression but was able to stay at a functioning pace and not take the small joys for granted. Once an extrovert, outgoing, fun, loving guy ready to talk to anyone pulling a one hundred and eighty degree turn to an introvert and isolating and keeping social distance and conversation to a minimal level. It really quite fascinated me to be honest with you, even if it had gone in the other direction in my case, it was part by choice, willing to live at the camp full time away from the city life and the rest of family and friends and part by circumstance. Would I have moved Sam and the two kids up there for them to complete their schooling and live out their childhood? More than likely not, so you start to think about really just anybody and do the decisions they make come about from choice, circumstance, some of both? I always heard the expression you get grumpier as you get older and it makes you think does someone roll out of bed and just say, "Yep, today I'll be grumpy."

I'm sure it happens but who could do that every day. I would think that would be exhausting. I imagine, in some cases, it's more of a slow morph over the course of one's life and a certain chain of events that dictates how one may choose to go about their business.

Zach's recommendation also focused on trying to get me to come back down to Troy and meet up with his wife and a friend that they would love to set me up with and felt like bringing back a dating interest would help ease some of the pain and get me back on track. I always declined and really did appreciate the offer and effort; they were at least trying and their hearts were in the right place. I just couldn't bring myself to consider it and kept telling him to stop trying but, I guess, that's when you realize that someone truly does care about you by continuing to try. He could have easily listened to me and just stopped and it was never extremely pushing just subtle messages or emails *"Hey, would love to have ya come down, we have a sitter, and we're going to have you meet so and so,"* never *"Hey, you need to get your ass down her and forget your dead wife and kids and start a new love story,"* kind of deal. First date would have been normal in the group setting but here's the second meeting talking about myself and loss of loved ones and replacing the only person I ever wanted to be with. When the idea doesn't even sound good or the possibility of putting yourself back out there isn't remotely enticing, why waste someone's time? I had the cool calming sounds of the water rippling off the lake in the summer and the warmth inside during the winter time, so I was all set.

Chapter 13
Unusual Migration

Another summer was upon us, the locals getting to their spring cleaning after the winter and tidying up the place for the soon to be influx of weekend warriors and out of town renters embarking on the small town and they wanted to put their best foot forward, as you would say. As this was an important time of year for local businesses and camp owners alike. The lake was skimmed over and checked to make sure the buoys were in the right place or if extra ones needed to be added. The marina would get their shipment of touristy merchandise like sweatshirts, tee-shirts, coffee mugs, you name it. Anything they could mark up the price by 100% for people who were on vacation and just let that credit card swipe away. The boats were usually the last thing to be taken out of storage because well-being at the base of the Adirondacks just because the calendar flipped to April didn't mean you were scot-free from old man winter or old person winter now to appease all parties. There were so called springs when you would think you were in the clear and start summer prepping in April then *wham*, close to a foot of snow out of nowhere, now a small silver lining that on occasion when that did happen, you knew you were not going to get a three-week freeze, like you would in January or February, so it was clear the roads and driveways and it would be back to spring after a few days. Extra shifts would soon be available for me to start my summer savings program to get me through the following winter on only a few shifts here and there and the store manager would love paying the extra wages but the bottom-line sales numbers increased his paycheck through the summer also. The surrounding camps around me would usually have a maintenance associate hired by the now camp owners; come check on the residences in early May to make sure everything survived the winter and there were no major repairs like fixing or replacing a dock, a new roof, pipes burst, etc., anything that would make renting out after Memorial Day that much more difficult. Most camps were winterized before December anyhow but still sometimes, a winter in the north country can be extremely fierce and all it would take is a pine tree falling in the right direction after a large snowstorm to completely wreck; a renting seasons income or ice falling from a tree and destroying an old ratchet-y dock that the owner has said they'll replace next year three years in a row.

Memorial Day usually signaled the start of summer in the North Country, usually the weather was cooperating by that point things were starting to liven up from the winter, kids were nearing the end of another school year, and people were ready to enjoy lake time. A heavy tourist destination usually helped kick things off about twenty minutes away from Chestertown at Lake George with a huge kick off to summer festival and this is when their local businesses usually opened and hotels booked up fast. Lake George was a larger lake and home to million-dollar lakeside properties in which the boat tours would casually motor by and give you a quick glimpse of what the elite looked like with these massive estates. Naturally, this festival helped kick off Chestertown's summer, as well being such a short drive away and anybody who wanted the experience but maybe didn't want to shell out the extra money for a hotel or own one of the Rockefeller lakeside properties, surrounding the lake would make camp in Chestertown. Businesses were out of hibernation and it usually seemed that the people were, too, they would take the winter months to relax and enjoy some peace and quiet and reboot their own systems. Catering to a summer destination crowd can be difficult. Sure, the money is nice and all but sometimes the reciprocation of even the slightest appreciation for your locally owned business is lacking and even downright ignored by someone just making it a weekend retreat or a week-long visit. You had to throw on your "customer is always right" smile and "thank you, have a great day" attitude because these people meant being able to maintain your livelihood for another season and if you wanted to go all high and mighty and slip in a go fuck yourself to an out-of-town patron, well, you certainly could do that. It was still a free country and freedom of speech was still at the top of the list but what wouldn't be at the top of the list was your business on the must visit list for goods and services, so, sure, sometimes the locals would fake it up and put on a nice charm. I got it and I always enjoyed sitting back and watching it.

The first week of June seemed to usually provide an uptick in traffic anyways after the holiday people would commonly make it an extended vacation if they didn't have kids or would keep them out of school for a long weekend. This wasn't terribly abnormal but heading into the second and third weeks usually provided a catch your breath moment for the locals since the previous summer and as they say, you can't just start a marathon by sprinting the first leg of it. This was always a welcomed little break and got everyone back on their toes and tiny glimpse of what the summer was going to bring. I noticed on my shifts that traffic was pretty abnormal during different shifts other than just the morning commute or afternoon drive home for work. This was out-of-towner traffic flowing more than usual and now actually started to include incoming families, not just the retired couples or the childless couples looking for a retreat from the real world. In most areas surrounding the upstate area and I guess there would always be a few exceptions but schools would normally not break for summer until the end of June to finish required testing and meet the minimum day threshold to keep all of their state aid and how many snow days needed to be taken during the fun months, so the school schedule remained largely the same from even way back when I was in school twenty something years ago.

"No vacancy" signs this early in the season at the local motels was also out of the norm and the local R.V. park that, again, didn't attract the snow birds back quite until the end of June in a normal year started seeing their season long renters coming back and setting up shop. You could feel a different vibe in the air over the course of the few weeks. It wasn't a calm welcome to summer and it's time for relaxation by the lake and retreat from the daily grind of the city life that had more of a rushed higher sense of urgency type of feel to it. The business owners loved it from the start, cash infusion to start June. This was fantastic, extra money to put away into the stash, and ensure a successful season and surviving the winter hopefully.

Cars that I never noticed before started making their entrances through the white pillars and settling at their camps and they weren't there to just open the camp's back up and check the grounds or catch an early weekend away before renting season would line their bank account. These were the actual property owners and it was like putting together one of those puzzle maps we used to do with the kids at the dining room table when it was raining to pass the time. New Jersey, Connecticut, Massachusetts, even saw a few southern states represented like Virginia and South Carolina. We knew this was likely going on, the original owners passed the properties down to a different generation that had different ideas of family values or sold them outright to settle an estate outright but it was interesting to see them congregate on the lake all at once at the same time. Maybe they were sent a private invitation by the Lake Charter to actually enjoy the perks of the lake life and enjoy the family atmosphere instead of cashing in to God knows who higher bidder for a week. There would be value in the actual owners using the properties more frequently as it would reduce the randomness factor and high turnover from week to week of people just spending money here and there. This would provide a real opportunity for consistent investment in the local businesses while maintaining a wonderful country atmosphere to bring your family. I am not sure if an email would have gone out or if something would have been snail-mailed, who knows maybe even a tax break would have been dangled to get the owners to rent less. The space for the building was running out and who knows what kind of creativity those geniuses were trying to drum up. It was interesting to hear and see the two beaches bustling before the July 4th holiday really implemented that it was time to cannonball off the dock and into the summer season. I even had to change my normal walking times to avoid the going/coming from the beach time, I would now hit the morning walk by 7:30 a.m. and my evening stroll after whatever ever delicious fine dining I crafted for myself around 6:00 p.m. or so, which was usually the peak dinner time and pre-campfire time so there was limited traffic say much lighter than between 4 to 5:30. Scott even called me and asked if I minded having my normal shipment of firewood pushed back a week so he could get smaller deliveries to camps. He wasn't used to dropping off this early in the season, I was understanding he always hooked me up anyways and I usually would have a little bit of reserved kept in decent condition under a small man-made firewood storage unit nestled between two pine trees, so it's not like my need was urgent but like many of the other businesses, Scott was in a joyful mood, getting this much action so early in the season, it was nice to see even for him being the rugged type. I joked with him if he was going to still let me shoot on his property or was he going to use that space for a nice coffee shop and offer mocha chai lattes with a bajillion sugars and free Wi-Fi. I actually only wanted to joke with him about that and not say that too loud because he could have easily sublet his land and sold to a high bidder but years of getting to know him that was not on the table at least for him.

My curiousness was peaked to see if this was going to maintain throughout the rest of the summer or was this a flash weekend type of deal, would we see the owners stay or would it be back to rent as usual? I knew what the businesses wanted having their appetites been given a filet mignon before the salad even comes out. Renters were usually easier to get rid of, too, they didn't linger, ask personal questions, try to get to know ya neighbor, and share a beer. I was way past that and got accustomed to the driveway wave or the friendly wave passing the beach but that was it. A weekend visit or a week-long visit did not warrant life story type of conversations, now talk about some of these people now staying for weeks at a time or heaven forbid, even longer like a month, then there would be more cause for interaction, they would see me at work, know what times I liked to take my walks and just overall be more curious, the latter would give me the night sweats and anxiety that I was not trying to introduce at this stage of my life. I tried to keep myself calm and not worry so much but it was going to be easy to figure out after a few weeks or so if the higher than normal traffic was owners of the camps or maybe there was a nice online magazine piece that I missed about the quaint little town of Chester providing an escape for all to boost tourism. Renters would never be at a camp for more than two weeks tops and that was really only due to two main reasons; one if they knew the owners well or were family, or two, if the owners had an extra week that was previously unrented, they would often offer a discounted rate for more time because greater than a dollar for the week was better than zero income for a week or a little less. More traffic on the tiny little dirt road and now more traffic in between camps for new to camp life children and curious camp owners. Some nights I just wanted to carefully place my shotgun on the back deck or by the fire pit as a nice, "Hey, don't wander through this camps trail again," never loaded, of course, like my brother and I would have stopped and said, "Aw, shucks," at a do not trespass sign or private property sign, so who would even know if the little rug rats of today would heed the sign and move on to another area?

The extra laughs at the beach and seeing the campfire flames, I guess, could have brought about some added happiness to the Marshall doom and gloom site and kick-started me back into being more outgoing and becoming more active in the community. I felt like I did my part and supported these places financially, kept my residence in pristine condition, even though I was barely hanging on by a thread emotionally, always paid the camps bills on time, and frankly, was why I moved up there in the first place was because the flow of traffic was so reduced compared to more southern in the Capital Region. I did not want this retreat to become like everyday life was there. You could only stay in the camp for so long, especially in the summer months because as nice as it was, sleeping at night you weren't installing central air conditioning units in the camps, so you were in a nice shady spot under a tree or trying to sit far enough back on the dock that a kayaker or non-motor boat enthusiast would start the small talk train from leaving the station and by the time you knew it, they were trying to make it a bullet train to information town.

We weren't even to the fourth of July yet and my sick of people meter was already teetering on the danger zone level of ain't gonna deal with it.

Even my relationship with Zach was starting to wane at this point in time and I guess I don't really blame him; a few years of refusing to visit him, his wife, and new baby in person or just come down and hang out for a few hours, he asked a few times if him and his family could spend the weekend at the camp and we could relive all of the great memories and rekindle a relationship that brothers are supposed to have but as we used to play WAR, it just wasn't in the cards for me. I would still text and email and get pictures of the family but I had set a pretty good defensive perimeter around myself and the camp as to not be intruded and I think he sensed that and there's only so many times you can extend an invite, hoping for a yes, but to be continually let down by the, "No, why would he waste any more time trying when he had his family to focus on and keeping them happy and providing for their brother?" or, "Not you only have so much time and effort after work and maintaining a healthy relationship with your partner and making sure you're being an excellent father," all the things that I cherished and I was truly happy for Zach but I wanted complete separation. God bless him, he even drove to the camp one Saturday during the winter, mind you, to try and straighten me out face to face but hearing it come from the mouth and not text message re-affirmed the point that he was going to have to stop trying and really wished I would come to my senses in getting older and such, we were pretty damn close to the only people that were left at this point. Accepting the death of loved ones, as you get older, feels more like the right part of life and lets you enjoy the memories that were created and shared throughout the person's lifetime. I had slowly been losing parts of my life now, almost longer than I have been alive and letting that sink in over a glass of whiskey neat will tear you apart. I still loved him a ton and wanted him to see my vantage point, as well that I didn't want to jump at the opportunity to see his now awesome family. I wasn't trying to make it a competition pity party like, "Oh, look at me, I've had way more people die than you."

He lost just as important people as I did less the immediate family and was hurting and trying to deal with grief just as I had been. Each grieves differently and maybe we just couldn't see eye to eye on why we were in a separation pattern but even flat out asked him what he would do in my position, now asking someone to put your shoes on is easier said than done. I already knew what stance he was going to have, "Get back out there, pick up the pieces, stay connected," and who knows maybe a lot of people felt that's what would have been best for me but deep down, knowing Zach, we were a lot alike and God forbid and he been in my position, I think he would be doing the *same* exact thing but when it's not happening directly to you and you can have your opinion, it will skewer your objectivity that way.

I stayed connected with him through a frequent Facetime call on the computer; a new program allows you to have a private video conference with whomever you wanted to invite in and could even invite multiple people in at once and made the old days of AOL instant messenger feel like you were still writing on stone tablets, just to see the kids and give a quick hello but our talk portion was always pretty brief and the same pleasantries. I only kept the Wi-Fi for the camp and was able to stream whatever I wanted to watch, which my interest in a lot of the things we used to watch like sports, now I hardly ever tuned in but would need something for the rainy and snow days to keep me busy. It would have been a pretty good resource for my parents and grandparents to use to keep us kids busy but we made due with puzzles and card games and as long as there wasn't any lightning and thunder present, you could even play out in the rain, who would have thought. I would always try and take the laptop outside on the nice days, a little better view than the urn paradise and liquor store vibe that I was able to turn the inside of the camp into.

Chapter 14
A Different Summer

Traffic through the rest of June remained steady which maybe everyone saved their vacation time up or the school schedule changed to let the kids out earlier in June now, who knows, but it was terribly surprising at this point because July 4th was always a big bash and seeing it stay pretty busy toward the end of June. Everyone just figured that it would continue into the July 4th holiday and then the locals would get their catch-up break to restock and take the mini-break before ramping up for the rest of the summer. Hearing late July or early August roars toward the end of June around the lake was a little bit refreshing, even though dealing with the crowds and working more was usually listed on the con side at this point. No one certainly was going to shoo the business away and I just tried to keep a smile and yes, after the 4th, we'll get our break before the rest of the summer. There is no way this traffic pattern will stay through the whole summer. Shopping at the local grocery store was now interesting as people were flocking there to stock up their camps, so I would shop first thing in the morning when they would open or would go late and weave in and out of the way of the pallets on the floor for re-stocking. I would pretend I was Jimmy Johnson racing in the Stop N Shop 500, grabbing all the essentials as I sped past with a cart that needed way more than an expert pit crew to patch up. One thing I would have to bribe one of the stockers I knew on the night shift, was the brother of the woodman and my shooting range hookup was toilet paper, he would make sure when I was going at night, he would keep a package in the back for me *(wink, wink)* and I would throw him a few shekels for his generosity. Man, these people were buying toilet paper like they owned all the stock shares in the company or they were nervous that the big bad toilet paper monster was going to come in the middle of the night and steal it all. Were they going to shit more during this vacation than they normally do at home? It was really baffling to me but it gave me something to debate myself out on the deck arguing that, yes, they absolutely needed to hoard all of the toilet paper and no, look around, do bears shit in the woods? There're enough pine cones to get the job done or if in an emergency toilet paper stop production, you just designate a tree that would give you the most privacy.

I certified myself as country now having declared that I had enough time at the camp as the primary residence and all the part time I had spent there and enough time away from the city life that I was, in fact, allowed to make fun of the city slickers working a canoe or buying all the cheater logs at the hardware store because they could not assemble and start a working fire, so they would buy them and casually drop at the base of the fire when no one was looking, so they were able to get the fire going and were the heroes of the night. I would always look up toward the sky and smile for my grandpa and just hear the step-by-step instructions he would give my brother and me to ensure we would always know how to start the fire, whether at the camp in our designated area or if we took a long hiking trip to be able to set up shop and camp for the night to keep warm. Self-proclaiming was fine there, no certificate needed or showing of birth records that you needed to be born north of exit sixteen of the Southway. I always joked and called it the Southway because the nickname for the actual highway we would take to get there was called the Northway so, naturally, when we were heading home from camp, which direction were we going in? I got my wooden Adirondack chair placed in a spot slightly further back than normal on the dock again with the increased traffic I was sitting back until the normal traffic pattern resumed for the July 4th fireworks show over the lake and this day would usually require a full bottle of whiskey and there was no mixer or chaser. It was pint glass, four ice-cubes, and pour away. While the fireworks show was always great, the day itself *always* brought back years and years of good times and thoughts of despair that I was sitting in a chair by myself without Sam sitting on one arm because these chairs were sturdy and well-built, so fitting both of us was no problem and usually the lake was kicking off its busy season, so the volume of people and families there to enjoy and take it all in hurt. Now this year, it was even busier than normal so stocking up for the bigger bottle was a must. This time, I didn't even look up at the sky to all the bright colors and different types of fireworks I looked down into my glass and then into a spot on the lake not occupied by a boat and watched the reflection in the lake until they were over trying to drown out the seemingly louder *oohh's* and *ahhh's* from folks. Maybe they don't get to see a lot of fireworks or since they were always renting to other people never saw this production. I would always sleep well that night for sure and would usually take a sick day following and hope for rain and just move from the bed to the couch and back to the bed as my daily activity. It was usually quieter the next day anyways because that was a pretty common trend with everyone celebrating and partying throughout the whole day. The 5th was always a recovery and relaxation day. In this instance, I was hoping that the Southway would be extra busy with everyone heading home after their nice little extended stay and boost to the local business and we could go back to our normal summer. I was secretly waiving the pom-poms next to the white pillars and channeling my air traffic controller skills directing drivers to make the turn left and head back to the highway, so they could head home and I could get my routine back and normal hiking trails that I missed so much over the last few weeks, and for the freaking toilet paper to not be bought out and having to bribe a stocker at the grocery store that could lose his job if he got caught.

Depending on how the calendar fell each year for the fourth, I would get a pretty good idea when things would return to normal, did the holiday fall on a weekend day where you would see the exiting traffic on a Monday or Tuesday, or did the holiday fall on a weekday where you typically see the traffic leaving on the following Saturday or Sunday, depending if they were owners and how far they had to travel or if they were renting what day their rental agreement was up? This year, the holiday fell on a

Thursday, so I circled Saturday and Sunday on my calendar clipped to the fridge and little smiley faces drawn on each day. There was no way these people were going to be able to stay any longer, right? They had jobs, kids played summer sports, shoot, they had homes or primary residences to tend to which, yeah, in the summertime, can be a little bit easier but they had to get back to their normal so we could get back to ours. I had a Saturday mid-day work shift at Landy's. Perfect, I would smile as the first wave of people who would be on their way. Nope, didn't happen as usual busy traffic people stocking up on gas and daily items, they might need instead of going to the normal grocery store for. Come on, a few hard punches on my way back to stock up the milk toward the end of my shift and the discouragement of taking the short drive back to camp. The night time was still busy, so I just sat on the deck and talked myself into Sunday being the day, made sense if the heavy traffic was owners of the camp anyways, then they aren't renting the camps stupid so, of course, they wouldn't have to leave on Saturday, but Sunday so they could get back home. Sunday departure was early mid-afternoon and definitely before dinner time depending on one's particular drive time. We would always head down a little bit later in the afternoon to soak up the last few hours of lake time but we also had a fairly short drive that didn't require four to six hours in the car so we could stay longer. How would I know if the Sunday departure actually happened? Easy, I would schedule my off-peak time hike for around dinner time, sometimes slightly after, and that would give me a pretty good indication whether it was a heavy departure day. I would actually take the main dirt road which would provide the best view of the driveways in most cases and even if it wasn't quite visible from the road, then just simply following the road provided a glimpse at the camp itself or the yard, or deck, basically, the back portion of the camp where I wanted to see lights off and no towels thrown over the deck railings for drying. A quarter of the way into the walk, I started to pick up the pace a little bit as the first results were not what I was hoping to see, cars still parked in the driveway, and thank heavens, my eyesight was still strong seeing license plates. I did not want to still see parked in the driveways. Halfway through my usual walk took me past the one beach that we always used to go, alright, no boats at the dock, no boats at the dock, and please, no people at the beach still. Great, check the no boxes to both of those, and the rest of the walk, while a few of the camps were in the condition I was hoping for, the overwhelming amount of the camps were still occupied. I even extended my walk a little bit because I was slacking the last few weeks so I surely needed it to take me past the other beach at this point. I was grasping for a sliver of hope. Nope, same thing just as busy and still bustling. I even called the wood guy on my slow walk back to my camp, like I just lost a high school football game to end the season to see if he was getting a lot of requests for drop offs today because Sunday was usually just that; he sure was as his voice seemed to jump a few octaves in excitement. I was going to be in the pretty small minority of people who wanted it to quiet down around the lake. I assumed the position on the deck in my chair and listened as the after dinner fires ramped up and the nighttime laughter was still going strong and I was slouched back just as I was the night before wondering what the next few weeks to months were going to bring about.

I was at least stocked up on the important stuff so I could keep my glass half full always and had a full beer fridge to outlast the unusual start to this summer, firewood was stocked and even if it got to low, there was some landscaping out front of a few small bushes that I didn't really like anymore that would have been good kindling and supplies were never the issue. It was the company and amount of people that was really bringing me down. The routine of saying hi and bye to renters was easy, this was shaping up to be a much different challenge than that and the amount of times changing my walking schedule or not taking as many work shifts as I normally would and sitting further back on the dock to not get approached by lake enthusiasts was going to be a tougher day to day ordeal that I never faced since making the camp my primary residence. I guess I could do more puzzles inside and keep the windows shut but again, going into July and August, that was brutal temperature-wise and at least I could sit inside naked if need be, they would more than likely frown upon that if I was doing that out on the dock or the deck, which, if someone was looking at hard enough from the water or had binoculars could get a pretty good view, not to say back when Sam and I first started going to the camp on random weekends off peak time before kids and all taking a dip off the dock *sans* bathing suit wasn't out of the question, but a little different scenario being young and carefree than being older by yourself in the middle of the daytime in usually a heavily trafficked stretch of lake.

I did clean the shotgun twice the week following the fourth since now I wasn't going to be able to head to the range and get the normal pre-peak season practice in, so I at least needed to make sure it was cleaned an extra time just in case one of these out-of-towner pieces of garbage felt like wandering through to the Marshall grounds. What was I in the old west and this was the O.K. Corral in Tombstone lining up villains (empty beer bottles) on the dining room table while I was spitting in my jar, telling the rascals to best be gettin' off my property 'cuz Betsy is nice and cleaned up and dressed to the nines to go out or in this case the twelves. I didn't even bother checking in with the actual people I talked to still in town since getting the giddy wood guy and even his brother was getting crazy hours at the grocery store everyone was, "Who cares? Let's keep this momentum going all summer long."

Yuck lake more like it if that was going to be the case.

Chapter 15
Christmas in August

I struggled through July as the businesses and lake continued to see the high traffic volume and seemingly more permanent at least in my view because they haven't left yet. Wonderful, they were enjoying their beautiful properties week after week and all the locale had to offer while I was falling asleep barely due to anxiety attacks and waking up from a dream in a cold sweat that there were a group of about thirty people just standing out on my back deck smiling at me and having a grand ole time firing up the grill and starting a fire in the fire pit. This was certainly happening throughout the pillar village as everyone was spending more valuable time together and making new friends each day and night. The rolling pin even made an entrance into the weapon cabinet and the chair on the dock was removed and placed back by the fire pit. I really needed to figure out why everyone was still here and why it wasn't the typical renter season yet, I fought to get my hands on a newspaper for thirty seconds while at work because people gobbled 'em up for a cheaper version of a fire igniter and the local paper at least would offer coupons for the weekly Stop N Shop ad. Hell, I even fired off a few texts to Zach to see how everything was going with him in Troy, and he relayed everything was "fine" and business as usual, wonderful, man of many words when I actually wanted to talk a Mr. Brokow news update with the hard hitting analysis *"We'll be back at quarter after for a live look at sports."*

Streaming the actual local news, nothing, interviews with local businesses gushing over this influx of steady ownership businesses and how thankful they were to have people staying longer and how greatly it was affecting all in the community in a positive light. That was it though, why, why was this summer so much more special? These people, I guess, had jobs or had everyone reached retirement age already that owned the properties or who felt like renting a motel room for three weeks or longer. It wasn't an unusual winter in terms of weather that people were so starved for warmer weather and the weather appeared to be pretty standard so far through June and through July nice and warm a few rainy days mixed in nice breeze at night to keep the camp windows open and perfect fire weather. I eliminated my morning time walk and really limited how far I wanted to travel for the evening version as well. I resorted to climbing the relatively short stairway in the back off the deck down to the fire pit area and turned a small spot in the garage into a calisthenics area to at least stay somewhat active and the stairs kept me outside to get some fresh air. I thought about maybe starting to jog or run again after a long layoff, so that at least the pace would be fast enough to eliminate a small portion of the camp population was completely out of shape to limit exposure to the, "Hey, how's it going?" and I would at least start by stretching in the garage, you know, you never just want to hit the road cold but having my stretching station located in the garage, which was where our beautiful old style refrigerator that I had pegged as a late '80s model that my grandmother thought would go perfectly in the kitchen now still serving its great purpose in the summer time of keeping the lagers cold and with the bottle opener conveniently hanging from a piece of rope which my grandfather would always argue definitely added some extra decor to the piece and one could argue served a more important purpose, although my dad would joke that he would just open it with his teeth if it wasn't hanging there and it usually led to the fridge door opening instead of heading out toward the driveway to start on my jog.

The national news was shifting toward heavy coverage of politics since it was now a big time election year and all the big ones were coming up in the next several months like the president, governor, races, house and senate seats up for grabs, so really anything unless catastrophic wasn't going to move the coverage away from who was in the front running in each race and what states were going to be vital for an individual to win to keep the momentum going. I would tune in briefly and then usually just mutter to myself that Paige was going to be the first woman president of the United States because shockingly in politics it still had not been a reality yet. I mean I could have just picked a driveway with an out of state license plate and knocked on the front door and asked why they were actually visiting *their* own camp right and why haven't they left yet. An even better idea was like how they take exit polls during the elections, just roam the beach and keep a tally of a few categories, "Where are you from?", "Why haven't you left yet?", and "When will you actually be leaving?"

Damn that switch to being an introvert and even after a few drinks, aka care inhibitors, meaning after having a few drinks, the filters come completely off. I just sunk into the comfort of the chair of choice and would go over imaginary results like I was giving a live update from the local firehouse which was where the people voted in Chestertown, "Alright, folks, I'm here live with some early polling results on *why* these people just will not leave and the overwhelming factor is they are just having so much fun and love the whole area and are just not ready to head back to their normal wherever is. Fuck my life, back to you, Marissa and Ryan."

I ended up cutting my hours in half again at Landy's to where I was almost working winter hours in the summertime as to limit my exposure to people as I wanted to try and curb the feeling of hate toward a group of people that we used to enjoy and embrace when the town was bustling with visitors to help the local economy. I'm sure there was another employee younger that needed the steadier paycheck or they could even hire one of the new locals because I'm sure they were going to work, and yeah, that is why I decided to cut the hours back because the train of thought usually started at Pleasantville, thinking of fond memories of meeting new people and learning their stories or using your imagination to come up with one for them, but then the train would quickly make a track switch and head right to Negativetown. I could ride it out, there was no way it was going into September because schools were starting back and traffic had to go back to normal, so whatever the infatuation was heading north, this summer was only a mere unusual turn of events. There was no way this would head into the fall after school was supposed to start and interrupt the beautiful scenery of the fall foliage that was amazing to view around town and through the mountains. I kept the train in Pleasantville for that one because it would have flown past Negativetown and more than likely ended up in the City of Anger.

Come on, August, this is our month. I woke up the first morning of the new month and actually enjoyed my coffee out on the deck and talked to the lake and said, "We're almost there. We'll be back to normal by the end of the month, vacations will be over, little Bobby and Jane or whatever the top ten names included these days, they certainly were not Bobby and Jane and even names like James and such were considered old school, had to be going back to school just remembering the local school schedules in the area started after Labor Day, so parents wouldn't rush back the night before school to get settled."

Some areas of the state would start at the end of August and different states likewise at the end of August; hence, my genuine optimism and I would be able to work full hours the rest of September and October to load up some winter pay. Labor Day normally landed very early in September in the first week; sometimes, it would drift into the ten-day range but if that was the case, then students would be back the week prior and just get the day off, so you could see why August was the month of joy. My hello waves and smiles now were underlined with goodbye feelings and "adios, thanks for fucking up this summer," but ah, well, one summer of abnormal was tolerable. I would be able to reset over the winter and get back to normal next year.

I kept pretty low key throughout August and felt like a child when we were gearing up for Christmas once the calendar hit December 1st, this was going to have the same feel. I didn't walk for about two weeks and just stayed at the camp and circled for the Tuesday after Labor Day as the day the running shoes would be dusted off and laced back up and I would jog around the lake like I was in contention for the New York City Marathon with my headband and shorty running shorts on. It was going to be magical! I made a special grocery trip and picked up a nice T-bone steak from the local butcher and a nice bottle of red wine. Sam and I would love our steak and wine nights out on the deck, I would have my grill apron on as I was the self-proclaimed grill master and she would always chuckle but I did cook a nice steak. We weren't wine snobs or anything and didn't really drink it often but it always gave us a nice feeling sitting out on the deck with each other and a nice steak and glass of wine.

I monitored the lake traffic through the last week of August since Labor Day was nice and early this year, which I hollered up a nice thank you to the calendar gods of September 3rd so, man, was I giddy about that last week, had an extra pep in my step and the only thing missing was hanging up the Christmas lights on the camp and dock which, don't get me wrong, I almost strongly considered doing after having my nightly meetings with Jack but that would have been too much work going to get them out of the garage packed away behind God knows what now. We used to decorate the camp for Christmas or have someone put them up for us when my dad or grandpa couldn't make it up there. Sam was always a fan of seeing it lit up with the snow-covered grounds and frozen lake, it really did look beautiful. I decorated the first and second winter I was there just to keep it almost like normal times and to get that feeling of joy but that waned and my interest in putting in the effort diminished down to not doing it anymore. Untangling used to generate some laughs, now it generated anger and stomping on the bulbs almost like you were popping bubble wrap. I wasn't completely full of Mr. Scrooge, yet I at least hung two wreaths each winter still one on the nice, red front door which looked awesome and then one on the door heading out onto the deck, so you could view from the lake. Shoot, I'm sure this week I was even wandering around humming some good ole Christmas tunes.

It was here at last, Labor Day weekend. The town busy, the lake crowded, fire pits surrounded, and sounds of camp goers ready to enjoy the last hoorah. The town just like July 4th would usually pick the Sunday night before because the majority of people were still around and wanted to give one last firework show to the people weather permitting of course. The weather Friday and Saturday were perfect like you took a drawing board and drew nothing but the sky with a few birds in it; a beach and the sun, you couldn't have asked for better weather, so, of course, after two days like that, being the professional weatherman I was for the lake, I knew that Sunday was going to be perfect also. Like most weathermen/women wouldn't, ya know it, at about 3:30 p.m. on Sunday. It was like someone flipped a switch from the beautiful paintings of Friday and Saturday and took a bucket of grey paint and dumped it right over the lake and turned the fan on high for the wind to pick up. Thunderstorms were pretty normal throughout the summer if we would get a lot of humidity in a particular stretch. This happened a few times before and unfortunately, it's not like the town liked postponing but that's exactly what they did, which is also one of the reasons they like to plan it on Sunday night, so they have an emergency back-up of Monday in case mother nature doesn't feel like watching a beautiful firework show that evening. *This would still keep me on track for steak date with myself for Tuesday*, I reasoned to myself, kids weren't going to miss the first day of school so by the a.m., I would be able to take the nice long walk or jog and really just see the close byers that had a reasonable distance to travel or didn't have kids to worry about getting back to school.

The show went off without a hitch on Monday after another picture-perfect weather day with all the *oohhs* and *ahhhs* one could imagine and sparklers by the firepits and the ice hitting the bottom of my glass when it was time to fill 'er up at the Marshall bar. The next day, there wasn't even going to be a hangover I was ready to wake up and see my presents in the form of empty driveways or at the very least, a vast reduction in occupied driveways. Early on started promising but about a quarter of a mile in my youthful enthusiasm quickly shifted to one of being dejected after not getting the one present that you put on your list that year. Car, car, car, it felt like I was playing duck, duck, goose, and I knew I was going to get caught any second because as the walk continued half mile, a mile and on the amount of out of state license plates and full

117

driveways was not the morning I had dreamed of. Like the many walks before and why I stopped walking or running as much seeing all of the families enjoying themselves and laughing and taking in all of the scenery, plus, I wasn't in the market for new friends. I couldn't believe I was slowly walking back to camp with the punch in the gut feeling again. I couldn't believe and talk myself into that, maybe it was just going to be another day or so until I would get my grounds back and everything would be back to normal. September and we were still where we were back in June. What the hell was happening, I didn't live under my camp and never come out, I mingled albeit very minimally at least it counted, were we in for a whole year of this? Were these people going to brave a winter, heck the majority of em probably didn't know how to put gas in a snowblower or ever shovel in their lives, there were a few contractors in town that handled camps but not to handle a volume of every day maintenance that these people were probably accustomed to. Plugging in all of their space heaters because they didn't have enough wood for a fire or stock up on pellets to keep warm so they would blow a fuse, smash, those thoughts put Marshall's bar down one pint glass.

Did you ever try and be a motivational speaker? Well I sure as shit was for the next ten days and hovered on cheerleader status making go home speeches to neighboring driveways and rah-rah-go-home now chants as I would see people enjoying lake time. It was not working, the town still crowded and it was time to prepare for the next quarter of unwanted visitors remaining potentially through the winter season which being completely honest hardly ever was done to have a high percentage of camps occupied during the winter months. The late summer nights that became some of our favorites was making a turn toward the dreaded Negative Town again really at this point I think I should have just changed my mailing address because that's where my full-time residence was. Not even the joy of football season was going to bring me out of this one. The feeling of hope sitting out on the deck at night or a rare night when I would start a fire hearing the same sounds again and again during a time that I frankly was not used to and especially, now did not welcome like; the solid wood that would keep the fire going for hours or enough time to hear a child finish a story. I grabbed the nice steak I bought after noticing and identifying that you cannot just chill a steak in the fridge for that long and chucked it like a boomerang right into the lake, the judges docked me a little on form but followed through and distance I aced. The wine stayed corked, I was mad, not to waste a good bottle of wine mad however.

I was unsure and unprepared to handle what I was going to do next; you psych yourself up so much and get ready for normalcy at a certain point after playing fake nice for a whole summer, which you never used to do but now have almost become a pro at. What was the next few days, weeks, and God forbid, more months of this going to do to me? I got my social butterfly wings from my dad and grandfather and had them enhanced by Zach and then flourished with Sam, that was eons ago and felt like ancient history. I didn't even want to wave at people anymore. I was Captain Introvert now and my super power was social distancing part by choice and part by life events. I usually enjoyed analytics with math and studying trends and this was now even entering the sports world as useful tools and strategy for teams across all sports, so I found it fascinating in that aspect and just using my general knowledge and kind of sorta, still knowing myself didn't need an advanced algorithm to come to the conclusion where this was going.

Chapter 16
Taking the First Step Again

The days blended together and before you knew it a month went by and just like the leaves creating a scene straight out of a painting of fall foliage; my hope for returning back to my normal was changing from hopeful to down right out of the question. Facing the reality of a more crowded village, like I was just defeated in triple overtime of a high school football game or losing a bet by half a point on a bad play that should have gone the other way and would have garnered a victory. Slouched in the chair like my dog just died, it wasn't like he just died, a few years and passed now but a simple look up to the mantle or a quick glance over at the bookshelf and there he was, with the rest of the family could garner some waterworks, just sitting there with the TV off and phone silenced unwilling to plug in, playing cards sprawled all over the floor like what would happen if Zach or I would lose game of *War* and puzzle pieces from probably four different puzzles spewed all over the table because I would now start a puzzle put a few pieces together, decide to do a mashup with a completely different puzzle, and you could have a loon sitting in the road or a camp sitting on top of the lake.

It was a great financial season for the local businesses but I hadn't ventured out at all to gather what their mood was like with the volume still cranked up to high with visitors. I imagined they were still giddy to stuff their pockets for a few extra weeks until the leaves fell and everyone made their way back home, so they could then hit the reset button and get some much-needed rest. The firework shows and flea markets and road races were now complete with no major plans because, well, usually, there isn't anybody left to put anything extra on for and it kinda had the mood of when a bar would flick the lights on and off signaling last call to scatter to the bar and get those last few drinks of liquid encouragement to make some bad decisions, so, of course, the visitors would get bored and definitely not want to stay for an entire winter. Swimming season was coming to an end but people would still flock to the beach and just take in the calmness of the water and the fires at night time were pretty spectacular with the leaves changing on the trees mixed in with the pine trees it was usually a nice calm and cool feeling to enjoy with limited other fire pits lit up, gave it a more unique feeling something that was only enjoyed by a special few. Sadly, sitting on the back deck, I didn't even want to walk down the stairs to the fire pit to start the fire as I would glance out and see almost a July fire pit scene; fires all around, taking in what we used to love doing in all the years at the end of the season, having one last weekend around this time before the winter hit. Marshmallows being roasted and stories being told around the fire with sounds of laughter rising, like the loon taking off from the lake to change perches and I felt the misery and despair starting to take over and just sat inside wondering why things didn't change mid-summer and why the white pillar village still was crowded and I was not going to get those answers because I wasn't going to ask anybody the questions.

Zach and I had a complete distancing and the only thing that kept us brothers was our last name. We were always so close growing up and now the one thing we swore would never happen had in fact happened; last I knew, him and his wife had two kids and he was doing extremely well for himself with work and they sold the Troy house and upgraded to a beautiful new house in Latham to accommodate the need for more space. He sent me one last email after so many attempts to stay relevant in my life with some of this updated information and I glanced through it and used the same delete button that I was an expert at using now, and probably didn't even know how to click on the reply button on my old laptop and my phone was still in service but it may as well as been deactivated because I didn't use it at all. There was a small path when you would open the side door, which would get you into the garage, that I would entertain starting on a walk or a hike to just get me out of the camp and get some fresh air to maybe shake the cobwebs and get my head right heading into the winter. I gave myself partial credit because at least I thought about doing it but it never materialized and I would just step back and close the door and turn the lock and retreat inside the camp. I was hardly sleeping anymore, dozing off for a nap here or there, or partially closing my eyes for a few hours mid-day. I would try and lay down but that just led to looking at the ceiling so I would just recline in the lounge chair or curl up on the couch that hadn't been upgraded in.

I can't tell you how long but they served their purpose. We would never buy new furniture just to put at the camp, the furniture upgrades would usually result from updating at their own home and instead of just throwing them out by the curb, we would throw them in the truck and deliver to the camp.

I would at least put a glass on the folding tray, we would station either next to the couch or the chair for our drinks or snacks, but the glass would remain empty and I took my swigs straight from the source that way. I wouldn't have to wash them each day and sometimes, I would pour it into a cup but that would occur in the morning with my coffee because everything was fine on lake time. What a beautiful thing now since I was such a valued customer at the liquor store, I probably helped send their kids to college. They agreed to deliver my order when I called 'em up, I didn't even have to dial the full number I had them as contact number one as Jack and Jim. I would scroll through some of the contacts from time to time after the call and one contact I didn't delete was Sam and it had a picture of the two of us that I always thought was one of our best pictures and even graced the cover of our wedding album, her sitting on my lap while we were waiting to be transported to our reception on a bench on a small flower garden and we have two of the most genuine smiles on our faces. I probably said something insanely corny but in that moment, it was so pure and real. Nights that were somewhat tolerable now were anything but as I would shut the camp and close all the windows to keep any outside noise out or at least make the attempt to but the laughter would stream through the old windows and right into my head. My head in my hands, sweating it out until 11 p.m., or so as now it would get a little chilly by that time and even with the fire going for out-of-towners, they usually didn't last much after that. We would be prepared and would have some nice handmade blankets and sweatshirts ready to go, so I just had to drown it out until then. Even pacing in front of the mantle and looking for answers with Dad and Grandpa for help produced no answers.

After trying my very best to drown out the sounds of the visitors and occupied camps throughout the days and laughter by night, this Saturday night was different. I forced myself to eat a peanut butter sandwich, as this was my fine dining now, but at least I was eating. The sun was starting to set over the same mountain located on the west side of the lake that we had a perfect view right from our deck and it was almost like a daily evening alarm, watching it disappear behind the mountain and watch the trees grow taller and fold into the night to head to the fire pit and get it all warmed up and chairs were being placed in their spot for the evening and the snacks and blankets were nicely folded waiting to be thrown over who called dibs on them first, or who could pry them away from whomever got them first. I couldn't stomach the thought of this continuing into November and December and heading into the following year with the same capacity and volume of people and no time to get myself right again reset for next summer.

Night time was upon us and I found myself in the garage with the side door open, glancing up at the old cuckoo clock that had the look of a bird house and even had chirping birds on the hour but now the chirping was disabled due to not replacing the batteries, so they would just judge me when I would hit the beer fridge, so the time was stuck on 9:10, so at least, it was right twice a day and this time. I didn't know if it was accurate or not by the darkness outside just being lit by some fire pits. It was likely to be a little later than that. Like the fire burning into the nice fall sky, the fire burning inside me now was kindled by anger and sadness; a deadly combination with a chaser of whatever the drink of the night was so throw some alcohol in the mix and we were looking at some pent-up emotion from quarantining myself for the last few weeks to avoid all contact. I had set out on that trail probably a thousand times over the years, which used to be a peaceful track that would give you a different vantage point of the lake without intruding on other camps grounds but also kept you off the main road to give you more of the hiking feeling, then just taking a stroll down the dirt road well-traveled on a daily basis. Where would the trail take me this time on this journey? What was going to be accomplished as I looked out and pondered about hitting the trail again and would I make any detours as the usual track would be fairly dark and this would surely create some panic if I had to carry a lamp or make sure my phones flashlight was working to guide me through some different trails that would in all likelihood with the population still high would cross me into a driveway or a fire pit area for sure. A fire pit area? That aroused my interest how about if the path took me toward a fire pit area of a nice family enjoying a nice fall evening fire, eating cookies and s'mores and telling campfire spooky stories maybe the story of the legend had made its way around the village, likely not because we had entered a time where you could not even scare your own kids and heaven forbid if you scared someone else's kids, even with a harmless ghost story without facing backlash and a fury of punishment. A sly smirk crossed my face thinking if my dad told his story now to some neighbor kids around the fire pit and a stern talking to from a parent would now turn into a call to the pine cone police or the F.B.I.

There was a shelf near the door and just under the now decorative not working clock. I couldn't venture out just like this with no face covering or bright clothes. I mean, even now the grey beard helped a little bit; was it going to be a short walk or was I going to unleash all the pent-up energy and maybe take the trails around the whole lake? There was also a small chance of running into a little bit larger of an animal, so a knife or some sort of weapon just in case was at least a good idea but wasn't a shotgun type of necessity. That shelf was the home of my snow removal gear so it was in the prime spot to head out this evening. I purchased a mask that was typically used for skiers but worked perfectly for my snow removal activities and for walks during the winter season, as well as gloves, two for two, lastly, a just in case weapon, a Swiss army knife was always stashed into the pocket of my black sweatshirt but was that going to be enough, I needed something else but I wasn't carrying a frying pan around. Just then it was almost like the sun had risen to show me what I needed to take, something must have crossed the driveway and set off the motion light which wrapped some light around just inside the door and there it was, the handmade rolling pin crafted for Sam's thirtieth birthday party that now, like the clock, was collecting dust and it definitely was not being used for any intended purposes of the utensil. It was just right in size in weight to be mobile but heavy enough to fend off some of the smaller animals I could encounter. If the path crossed with a bear, well, then, sadly, I would have had to channel my inner Olympian track speed which was never there to begin with. It was a slim possibility which would hardly happen with how populated the lake and woods had become. They sought refuge elsewhere but from time to time, you would get a wanderer.

For the first time in what seemed like forever, I took that first step out of the garage door uncertain on where the path would lead me or would I venture off the well-known path and create a new one with footprints more angrily placed in the soon to be hardened ground with the first frost approaching. I set out through the trees without a plan, curious and cautious all at the same time, would the path take me too close to another camp enjoying the nice evening and how would I react if it even brought me face to face with a family. I needed to get out and it was almost like someone was standing behind me in the garage and pushed me out for extra encouragement. With the mask on and lack of exercise, I was breathing heavier than normal but was walking at a slower speed, you don't kick the athletic muscles back into gear after thirty steps so slow and steady wins the race with my dark clothes and rolling pin. If my dad and grandfather could see me now, they would have rolled down the slight embankment and even may have rolled all the way into the lake overcome with laughter at my fierce look. My first break leaning up against a tree, hoping they weren't rolling over in their respective urns but I didn't care. This was needed for my sanity's sake since the daytime didn't offer me one ounce of solace. Tortoise pace but so far so good, trek was good and most importantly, no sign of a clear path leading directly to a camp, each breath leading to more confidence and focus to keep going and feel like normal again.

I wasn't tracking my distance or time because my body was going to tell me when I should retreat back to camp as my legs and back would get a little heavier. I didn't make any random turns and stayed close to the known path for this first venture out and decided to make the U-turn now and plan to set out for tomorrow night around the same time with a feeling of accomplishment from this brief walk back out to get some fresh air. The next day was cloudy and not as nice as the previous day, so as long as a late season thunderstorm didn't roll in and it wasn't monsoon raining, this would be a good evening to take another walk as this would limit the number of people wanting to be outside surrounded by a fire, as it was getting colder at night on the good days. A day like this; it would be pretty bitter at night so I was anticipating venturing a little bit farther like Zach and I used to test our limits when we were just boys seeing if we could keep going until we couldn't hear Dad or Grandpa yelling for us and sure a time or two, it led to a very stern talking to if we went outside of yelling distance but as long as I didn't leave Zach by a tree or something, he was usually okay with us venturing out a little bit as we got older. With the thought of having a little more freedom on this night, I was planning on making a few different turns to test the boundaries of where I would actually be able to go on the nice nights remaining with the ultimate goal of steering clear of driveways and firepits. I was able to start slightly earlier with the clouds still covering the night sky and the moon barely visible, so I took the steps out of the garage again with the same protection. I felt like an aging ninja ready to attack in the night but instead of nun-chucks or a samurai sword, I had a rolling pin which totally took away some of the cred for carrying the Swiss army knife.

Same path and same results so far with just enjoying the pine trees still traveling at a nice and steady pace as to still allow my body to come out of hibernation of inactivity and to sweat out the Jack and Coke from the afternoon happy hour reaching the tree that I made the U-turn at the night before and standing straight up with my arm barely resting on the rough bark deciding that I was going to keep going and try to explore a different path and mark some trees with the knife if they lead to a danger zone, driveway, or firepit and using my analytics on this particular night worst case scenario had a very minimal chance of leading straight into the fire of an unsuspecting camp owner or permanent visitor. I made the right turn on this night as this path kept me clear of all camps and kept the Swiss army knife in my pocket until I was ready to turn around and head back to the camp after walking farther than the night before and after marking the tree at my turnaround spot with what was my best attempt at making a J looked like a four-year-old was being trusted with a Swiss army knife.

Chapter 17
Trail of Rage

The clouds stuck around for another day so I decided to give myself a nice deserving day off as they often say when getting back into fitness; it was usually a wise move to break it up and not start out to vigorously or one's risk of injury went through the roof. Even though this was walking, it wasn't on solid pavement and presented some challenges and in fact, looking back, I even believe one night when we were younger, we had a pretty good crew at the camp for my dad to scare and he wanted to take full advantage, so he started out with his normal routine but this time, he wanted more flare; more than likely, the adult afternoon happy hour started a little earlier that day so he went to circle around the camp and wanted to make a surprise entrance through a set of trees just located to the right of the firepit if you were facing the lake and sure enough, he tried making a lunging step and instead of the usual loud fierce call, it sounded like someone was dying not from the legend but a torn hamstring. Gotta stretch those hammies kiddos and adults. It was a great laugh, then seeing my dad with a bag of ice secured under his leg and also quite comforting because he did a pretty number on it, so we knew we had at least a few more nights off if not the remainder of the week from him trying to scare us.

A slightly overcast start to a Tuesday but turned out to be a nice day, heading to dinner time, so the trek was still going to be on tonight and we would see which way I would want to go. The nights remained pretty consistent temperature-wise with no real threat of our first snowstorm, so I was able to mark some different trees hopefully. I took a late nap and woke up and got my bearings straight enjoyed some time sitting out on the deck as the evening set in and I just happened to peek at my phone for a time reading and it was 9:04 p.m.

Oh, the clock was almost right as I opened the door and put my mask on. A slight tap on the first tree I marked with determination to head out and explore some more. I reached the point where on the cloudy night, I decided to head down a different path and feeling a little bit more adventurous, I was going to head in a different direction this evening as well, gamble a little to maybe try and carve an M on a different tree this time around and expand on paths that may be useful at a later time.

I was able to put some slight markings on a few trees as it started off just as peacefully as the other night and my mind relaxed and then, of course, wouldn't you know it, one more step and I would have stepped right into the firepit area of another camp, a drop of sweat beaded down my forehead and landed on the mask and letting out a sigh of relief that a fire was not burning. Luckily, they must of been waiting for a wood delivery or was just enjoying some comfort inside because I would have surely been seen and I don't know who would have been more spooked me or the camp goers. Taking the different turn, I had to know would bring about this higher possibility more, so I used more discretion and not just plowing my nice hiking boots that Sam had gotten for me years back that were still almost like new due to my recent lack of exploring. I got pretty lucky because this venture this evening brought me to more camps than the previous night, so this was a good learning walk. The tally reached four and then a driveway in which I was able to sneak around and nobody was having a fire, so I would try and make a visible mark on them the best. I could to hopefully give me enough of a warning for future hikes to turn and head in a different direction. After the driveway, I felt that was a close enough call so I b-lined it back to the trail and got back to camp feeling like I just survived a mission impossible heist; throwing my mask and barely kicking my boots off in time before entering the camp and huffing and puffing back to my chair to rest for the evening. I was going to lay low for a few days after walking what I believed would have been a few miles and was a good start and something to build on.

I set the next one up for Sunday and would look to take a longer path, weather permitting, and it set up pretty nicely; plus, you had to avoid the busy campfire nights of Friday and Saturday and especially after this Friday, which was a washout, so Saturday was going to be an extremely busy night out. I sat out on the deck on Saturday and watched as the firepits lit up like it was a fucking night in mid-August, making mocking laughing sounds and mimicking other campers joy by the fire, "Oh, darling, how funny you are, what a silly story,", "Oh, my love, how wonderful this is with the children huddled around the fire and the love of my life right next to me."

Puke. Bottles up that night for sure to drown that crap out and suppress the anger that I felt. Big Sunday dinners to keep families inside longer with the hopes, leading them right to bed instead of outside to start a fire, their bellies too full to be woofing down s'mores and other snacks during the fire time.

I felt like Clark Kent heading to the phone booth to change into his superman costume. Only mine was in a garage and was dark and instead of a cape, I put a mask on shielding my face, so it was just slightly different. Same start down the path into the woods to see what adventure we could get into tonight, figured everyone went pretty strong Saturday night, so by this time at night on Sunday, the same thing that happened the other night would produce the same results if my trail led to more unmarked trees leading to camps or driveways. This night would turn into a far cry from anything feeling like Clark Kent. I took to the trail at a decent walking pace and a feeling of excitement being back out in the peaceful woods again by myself, breathing in the fresh pine tree smell, and the freshness of the air that you couldn't even make an air freshener to replicate it. I heard faint laughing on the last walk but not nearly remotely close enough to trigger any emotion and it was far enough off in the distance to not pose an immediate threat of being uncovered. This night was not how I envisioned it going at all and after the initial known trail where I would not be crossing into unknown territory, the sound became more prevalent like I was heading closer to a lightning strike. Dad and Grandpa were almost like storm chasers; not they would ever take that great of a risk but they would hear the boom of the thunder in between lightning striking and would make the calculation if it was a hurry up and scoot storm coming or we could take a few more plunges of the dock before retreating inside off in the distance type of storm. Sam would be a little bit more on the adventurous side and she actually enjoyed when the rain would first start to fall and everyone else around us was heading to shore, we would stay just a tad bit longer and enjoy some alone time in the lake but then once we had Paige starting to tag along no way, every thunder boom was a hurry up and scoot back to camp storm, hurry, back up the deck, and inside the camp quickly.

What the hell with these people! I was going to have to call the wood guy up *pronto* the next morning and have him start giving me a weekly delivery schedule to these people, so I could plan my walks better because on this night, the sounds of laughter, oh, were they ringing loudly off the tall pines. I would have to mark trees a little bit farther back but this gave me a sense of direction at the very least and after a while on the walk, I felt something change and instead of changing course away from the sounds of people enjoying the night out either on the deck or by the fire, I found myself walking toward it. Gone was the feeling of timid of the next step possibly leading to being seen, I was able to listen and tactfully plot my course on the fly and mark a tree where it needed to be at a safe distance or take an extended peek at the layout of a firepit area and what was the quickest way to get to the firepit area if I stumbled upon a driveway. I hadn't sensed this feeling of excitement in a while and didn't take a break at the tree to try and dig a little deeper as to what made the switch flip to not caring about where this next path would take me or what mental picture of a car's license plate being from out of state place; a sly smirk on my face eagerly slicing a mark in the nearest tree that a camp goer would just assume a bird or some type of the local wildlife was the culprit.

My ears had it pegged as a couple as the sounds were more mature and wine giggly than youthful laughs and I stationed quietly at a tree and squatted to process any information I could gather, *Where were they from? Were they talking about leaving anytime soon?*

My eyes confirmed what my ears relayed and it was a younger couple and I was positioned good enough to hear the conversation and instead of marking the tree and leaving, I stayed, quietly awaiting the information I was so desperate to hear "This is such a great last night here, but I am excited to get back home tomorrow."

The conversation back and forth was about how lucky they were to have this place and they were looking forward to many more trips in the coming years back here and that they couldn't wait to bring their family and have little kids running around. Head down and shaking back and forth the conversation became muddled and like a traffic signal going from green to yellow to red, I went to red in what seemed like an instance and what happened next was the anger rising to the surface as I closed in on the noise and soon found myself standing over the back of two nicely crafted Adirondack chairs enjoying a nice fire and two swings later, bodies on the ground motionless like a fish that finally realized it was not going to squirm its way back into the water off of the dock. I don't know why you wouldn't just want to go home. I am sure it was a lovely home instead of spending your time here and in my space but I was relieved and exhaled that thankfully I helped rid the village of people there to tarnish it.

I was surprised by my creativity for the next steps as I had not planned on this walk going this way but I managed to get them in the trunk of their car, drove the nice sedan with the Connecticut license plates back to the Marshall Camp and cleared enough space to park the car in the garage so if someone peered into my driveway, they wouldn't be alarmed by another car actually in my driveway after it being a one car lane for so long. I was going to take the car to the impound lot with all the tags and stickers removed after a good cleaning and give a Benjamin to the manager as it was a nice BMW sedan that I was just going to say that it was a gift from a deceased relative that I wanted no part of the vehicle, with the type of car and what they would be able to do with it, the questions were left unasked and they gladly took the keys.

I felt invigorated and energized and hoped that the next night would be as productive as the previous one. I had a bounce back in my step and an eagerness to head out onto the path again, not solely focused on the markings to shy away from a camp but sought them out to guide me to a camp. The car probably wasn't the best idea but by the time it was sold as is or broken down for parts, enough time would have passed and the guy at the impound, would have made a good buck and plus my tip was made whole I probably would leave the vehicle the next time. Pristine weather the next day and a smooth transition into the sunset and I even treated myself to a steak dinner, delivery, of course, from The Laketime Restaurant, still family owned and running a very successful catering/delivery service to keep up with the times and ever-changing restaurant guidelines for how many people could be in a confined smaller space at one time. The business model needed to be changed or there would be another mansion camp built on the site. They stuck to the years of hard work they put into the place and I admired them for that, so I wanted to support them and support the delivery service every so often.

I devoured the perfectly cooked medium New York Strip with a nice garlic butter sauce on top and went to the chair to get ready to head out for the nightly walk, which was shaping up to be a nice night out. The darkness settling in and my antsiness growing, I headed toward the garage and suited up and hit the trail. Modest amount of light guiding the path and some sounds of laughter ringing through the night sky again, I leisurely strolled and enjoyed the darkness of my new feelings and not wanting to shy away from them but embrace them. Perfect! I extended the trail again and was about twenty yards away from another firepit being occupied on the nice evening. Parents and two teenage children, so I squatted down to do the recon on the story and listen for the answers I wanted to hear, "Glad we packed everything earlier so we can stay up later tonight and just hit the road tomorrow, Susan,", "But, Dad, can't we just stay a few extra days, we will make up our schoolwork. I promise,", "Sorry, Charlotte, no can do, your studies are not to be missed." Disappointment once again as the conversation again wandered down the how lucky they were and so happy to have their family here.

No shit, geniuses, like I didn't want my wife and kids, who just by glancing and putting my head down to its proper shaking position back and forth, would have been pretty close in age to the two sitting by the fire with their asshole parents. I walked out from the trees, standing at six feet two inches, I was surely tall enough to be seen over a decent size fire and I felt as tall as the beautiful pines and as one of the flames readjusted, I made eye contact with the father who seemed to flinch slightly and that's when I made my move toward them quickly and engaging with one fell swing across his head and then back up across the wife's head as the daughter sat mortified; the son getting up to retrieve his phone sitting on the deck as I close in on him, swipe his leg, and finish the job while the daughter had now passed out with all of the excitement noise was minimal with the crackling of the fire and birds that hadn't taken their normal winter vacation yet.

An old SUV didn't have the same retail value for discrepancy at the junkyard that a BMW did, so they were going to take a nice winter swim, quick check of the license plates, and sweet victory Massachusetts, I guess maybe taking or trying to take a quick glance if I could before jetting out would have been a wiser move but they must have been implant Mass-holes because when they were talking about parking the car, it wasn't, "Ya, real glad we got tha cahh all loaded for tommarah."

Another solid stroll back to camp and a quick wash, the garage was the place of vintage appliances like my ever-popular beer cooler, there was a G.E. washer dryer set hooked up so we didn't have to go to a Laundromat or anything like that and wear and tear on them had been minimal so they were still running strong. The dryer was hardly ever used because we would just be able to string the clothes out on the deck during the sunny days of my new hiking garb to rinse all of the sweat out, or that's what I was telling myself, but I would be the first person to be sweating blood that way they'd be ready for the next adventure.

The next few weeks were profoundly better. I didn't hit the walking trail as much as we were getting a little chillier by the day and some late season rain storms which where we were could turn into snowflakes at a moment's notice, so I took the opportunities to hang on the deck and watch the birds start leaving their summer home and heading to whichever southern state they resided in during the winter. I, personally, loved the idea of the Carolinas just far enough away to avoid an abundance of snow but Florida would have generated a nice warmer climate so I often wondered and would try and guess which flock was headed here and Swish and I would play air traffic controller, "Alright, flock number six five three, you are now clear for takeoff."

Swish thought he was the pilot, whatever. I wasn't going to fight him on it, *"Roger that, ATC, confirm ready for takeoff."*

I geared up with some warmer clothes as the nighttime was getting a little more brisk so I would add another shirt under the black sweatshirt and some heavier socks, boots were solid, and of course the facemask was built for a skier anyhow, so we were golden, and just the last piece was some nice gloves that were pretty flexible and not too bulky for the intended use. I started wondering why the locals didn't step up and raise some concern over everyone staying for so damn long and well, I knew the reasons, so they could

140

stuff their profits and brag at Landy's how their profit margin was doing and they were going to go on a ten-day cruise early next spring, so I was gonna hit the trail for a known camp on the board. They let this happen and I was going to make them pay; one in particular who, for whatever reason, would give us a hard time every time we were there who like us inherited the camp but I don't know what her parents told her about the Marshalls but you would have thought by the looks we would get and the stuck up nose the we were in direct relationship with the mob. We would always add fuel to the fire though and wave and yell loudly over to her nice spot on the beach asking how they were doing. She had a husband but through the travel up lake news, especially when it related to lake news, they were now divorced and she took her throne on the lake board to rule. Not that I would admit to it or anything, but Zach and I might have toilet papered some trees and ruined her perfect tanning spot by having to run the perfect football route right by here splashing some sand up. This gave me the perfect knowledge on how to trail through the night and make my way to her tree line; one car in the driveway lights on and no fire outside, perfect, we were clear for takeoff and one nice thing up here you wouldn't have to worry about digging and turning up fake rocks around the driveway or decorations on the deck especially of a local because things hardly ever got locked, so I made my way to the rear of the camp where two large bay windows gave her a nice view of the lake but also was on the second floor and on the first ground level was a sliding glass door that was dark at the moment, so I snuck up to the door and wouldn't you know it, she locked it. Of course she did, I wasn't just going to venture to the front door, ring the doorbell, and ask for some sugar or ask her out on a date or anything. Trying to glance up to any doorway, I might see that could be wired with a motion light trying not to step on every single pine cone on the grounds. Jackpot! A door on the side of the building, no light going off after gently waving the rolling pin in what I assumed its target radius was, briefly grabbing at the door handle to see if this was going to be an easy turn or if the army knife was going to have to make an appearance. This freaking woman locked in Carol, I nicknamed her, all well good thing. My Dad showed me how to use this thing for this exact purpose just in case all of our doors were locked at the camp and needed to resort to hacking in. It was almost like one of the accessories was built for this exact purpose and it probably was but again the locks here were not sophisticated like I would see infomercials for now; you lock the door with your eyes and press your thumb on the door handle to unlock it and if someone not registered enters, an alarm goes off. That technology stayed out of the camp village and thankfully so, easy lock to manipulate a simple entry of the tool and swift turn at the same time and minimal noise, I was in what looked to be a mudroom that thankfully had another door that was shut to help prevent me from being seen to quickly and also plot quickly best course of action. It also sounded like the TV was on so that would give me a nice blanket for any noise that would sneak out before I would have it under control. A few trips back and forth by what I could sneak a peak of just under the doorway and I had to assume that was going to be my best chance on one of the next trips by to either a bathroom break or maybe she forgot something out in the kitchen, so I was ready, but that was it no more trips past and to make matters worse, the light was turned off and I now panicked with some curse words under my breath to her about doing this.

After the background noise of the TV vanished, it appeared as if she was headed to bed and this was going to be another adventure for me because I doubt, I was actually ever inside the camp and was unfamiliar with the layout on where the queen rested. Plus the issue with my boots; it's not like I was trying not to make any footprints but this was a whole new ballgame entering a residence, so I quickly flashed my phone to take a peek where exactly I was and look for a miracle that this was a partial supply room also. Poof! Garbage bags right on a shelf near the door, so I quickly chopped two up and stashed the remains right in my shirt pocket and covered my boots and tucked the overflow right into the top, securing my overlapping pants. A test of the door to check the potential noise factor and since it was probably used often opened slowly and quietly and even better news, there were two night lights placed in what I could tell was the kitchen straight ahead and a downstairs bathroom to the left. I tiptoed quietly down the left and there was in fact a bathroom located there with a bedroom unoccupied because why would she be in the first room, so I backtracked past the mudroom and veered into the living room and located a stairway going to the upstairs portion of the camp. A final deep-ish breath before I moved gingerly one step at a time as to not make too much noise with my awesome new homemade slippers that I'm sure you could buy on QVC because they were so chic looking but right now on the carpeted stairs, they were serving the purpose. I almost wondered aloud how many bedrooms were up here and then a gift of a clue was delivered, sound of water running from the end of the hallway which I presumed was the master bedroom with a bathroom for her highness to gracefully get ready for the night's rest.

I left the rolling pin perched outside by the door. As entering the camp, I needed to be a little bit more mobile and the army knife gave me a last resort but with the gloves on, we were going to go another route. I waited for the light to be turned off and pipes still making noise gave me a cover to sneak down the hallway and peak through the half-opened door just in time to catch her take her spot in bed and I waited cautiously for a while to make sure there wasn't going to be any more trips back to the bathroom or she forgot something downstairs. All clear, made the move and took care of business and gently affixed the body to make it look like natural causes and hightailed it outta there and back to camp while my adrenaline was higher than one of the fireworks shot off during the summertime events. It felt like it took me only three minutes to get back to the camp.

Chapter 18
Panic through the Pines

Stretching my arms out after sitting up in my bed, yes, the bed, I was sleeping comfortably back on the bed and getting good sleep through the night and would do the morning check on the pellet stove and refill as needed as the coffee pot percolating to get the day off to a nice start and a sense of relaxation as we were trending to the winter months and a much harder trail through the woods so I was going to camp and hibernate through the winter and continue my isolation and come out in the spring ready and even more refreshed and looking forward to checking out more camps and what levels of occupancy still remain. I set to winterize the camp, make sure there was oil in the snowblower and gas ready to go, fresh stock of pellets, winter clothes out in the spare bedroom and summer clothes sprawled in the other room as I heard Sam barking from the kitchen telling me to fold them and put them away. There was no reason for such organization and these rooms in my opinion served as the perfect clothes storing spaces.

The all-important winter delivery from the liquor store and several cases of beer from the local brewery of my favorite suds was delivered to the driveway and loaded to a short-term resting place in the fridge. The ultimate goal of minimizing grocery trips and guess what they even delivered now, what a world, so I placed my order online and for a slight delivery charge, *poof*, groceries in the driveway being placed right in my garage to bring into the house. I would stock up and freeze what I could for duration purposes and would only need the delivery of eggs and loaves of bread but the cabinets received a bountiful supply of soups and snacks, water supply was never an issue as the camp village was hooked up for public water lines, which was always a blessing, so now a water filter placed in the fridge to keep the water nice and cold which was always a funny little debate Sam and I would have; she loved her bottled water and drank it at room temperature. I couldn't believe this, not so much at the bottle water portion but did you ever say to yourself on a warm summer day, "Wow! A lukewarm bottle of water sounds delicious, darling. Could you get me a bottle from the garage?" which was where in fact it was stored when we would make our trips there as we would usually buy a few cases.

A trip to the garage to gather some brews to stock up inside and just glance over to where my winter boots were and looking at the shelf where my mask and gloves were kept immediately turned to panic as there was something missing that was now a permanent resident, good thing all of the doors were shut because the volume of, "Shit, shit, shit," quickly blurted out and frantically tearing the garage apart just hoping I knocked it off the shelf in a drunken stumble or I was fooling around with it inside like it was a ninja sword. I turned the search to the inside just to make sure I wasn't using it like a teddy bear maybe that's why I was sleeping better. I was using a damn rolling pin as a sleep aid.

"Sam, have you seen the rolling pin?"

"No, James. I have zero clue what and where you had it last."

Damn, damn, damn, we often played a game of hide and go seek with household items and would bicker back and forth that it was the other one's fault and nine times out of ten, it was sure my fault. This was a little bit more of an urgent search sometimes if we deemed the item non-essential, we would just shrug it off and go on about our daily lives. I lifted up the chair and couch, then crashed in the chair to gather my thoughts, and try and trace my steps back to where I had it when the small light bulb went off in my dumb head.

I waited until it was dark out and set out on a search and rescue mission and hoped it was still where I left it before entering the chairwoman's house. Her death was in the local news and to my knowledge, there was no suspicion of foul play yet anyways until someone else potentially found the rolling pin labeled with my family's initials carved in the handle nestled by one of the trees before getting to the camp. I surveyed what I could and walked cautiously to ensure nobody was there and they're definitely wasn't a fire going and it appeared there were no lights on which afforded me the opportunity to follow the same path, varying the exact steps as to not create another footprint, and kept to the tree line and maybe look like someone was exploring a random trail or got lost and needed to cut through the property lines. In this part of the state, we were fast approaching our first snowfall and some years, it came in like a beast to upward of a foot of snow dropped on us by November. I needed this to not happen then I thought no that would be good. I'll get the rolling pin back to camp and the ground would be covered in snow for the next five months. Making my way around my camp to the door, I entered on that night to where I left the rolling pin and a worse expletive escaped my mouth under the mask because it wasn't there. Did the big bad chipmunk take it back to his home so he and his family could bake cookies all winter? Was it one of the last rainstorms where the wind picked up pretty heavily at times and blew it around somewhere? It was dark and the lighting was poor so an expanded search was not going to be an option. I quickly checked a little bit farther away from the camp by about fifteen steps or so, as that was all the light the moon could provide before the tree line hit and I didn't need to be glaring at my cell phone flashlight or another small flashlight around the camp.

I was going to have to stage a daytime visit to recoup the rolling pin and with sunrise right around 5:15 a.m., I needed to get there right around that time as traffic would be light and everyone would still be sleeping. I got back to the camp pretty late and I probably only slept about what felt like fifteen minutes as I rocked anxiously in the reclining chair in the living room, racing my mind, and plotting where I needed to search on where the rolling pin could have gone after the night I was there. My right leg was bouncing up and down with anticipation as the bright yellow thing finally started to peak its head out through the trees and the clock confirmed what I now needed to go do as my only mission. I dressed a little more friendlier just in case anyone was walking by I could stumble my way, through as to why I was near the camp, through the trail and at the spot where the initial investigation began. I scanned the tree line and thought I would start there to keep cover and maybe it did get blown into the woods, that would have been perfect as the trees provided good cover and I wouldn't have had to step out in plain sight as the sun continued to climb over the trees. The birds provided some sound cover as they were usually pretty talkative in the morning so as I cracked on the fallen pine cones, I weaved in and out of trees, looking for the rolling pin. The tree line being my favorite option produced no results and I was on the other side of the property and now I had to game plan the next search radius. I needed to try and keep this somewhat organized instead of just sweeping back and forth in random spots to make and major trails on the property, so I got to the edge of the tree line and worked my back to the other side and maybe a pinecone stopped it before rolling all the way into the woods and would sweep the area like that and hoping that getting close to the camp wouldn't happen. Back and forth, back and forth what seemed like one hundred trips, not in the fire pit, not under the deck. I had to get back closer to the door where I entered the camp and maybe I just couldn't see that well the night before. I sneaked to get a quick peek at the driveway to make sure there was no car there of a family member that maybe would be there to clean the camp, gather belongings etc.

All clear, I didn't mess around with the tree line this time. I took a straight line right to the other side of the camp and practically dove on the ground by the door and started scanning the area by the door walking out away from the camp, nothing. After what seemed like five years frantically searching, I took a seat on the ground by the door and put my hands in my head and figured this was it, someone found it and they are just running the prints and matching the initials to property owners and gathering a list of renters down at the deputy's office to have a strong enough case for prosecution. I had a good run and what was really the point anymore, not like I had anybody to go back to the camp to, *come on, come on, snap out of it. That's dumb talk, get your shit together and find this freaking thing.*

Right as I'm about to stand up, I look to my right and in some camps, if there was no basement, if it was on a hill or whatever there could on the other side of the camp be a lower level, in which case, sometimes, the camp would not be set on the ground and this was the case for this particular property, what do I see? The handle of the rolling pin resting comfortably on a cinder block just under the side of the camp. I look around and make sure the coast is still clear and then I hear an unexpected sound from inside the camp, *What the hell is that*? as the sound was getting louder. It was the garage door opening, who the hell was there? Were they there last night, too, and parked in the garage? Who the hell parks in the garage up here anyways? Damn it, I couldn't risk going to grab it because that's where the garage was and I would have been walking right to the noise and there definitely was not enough room to get myself covered or shielded until the car ran away, so I quickly scooted back to the tree line and took cover behind a random woodpile that I would guess was being saved for a fire as I kicked the tree in front of me. By now, the sun was practically serving as a spotlight and I couldn't risk being seen by people out on their morning walk.

I knew where it was and I knew I had to get back there right at sunset to get the damn thing; even if someone was still saying at the camp, it was still there so clearly no one had found it yet, which gave me an ounce of hope and feeling that I would have it back to its proper spot shortly after sunset. The coffee couldn't brew fast enough as I now had to sweat out the rest of the day and then at about 9 a.m., damn, that clock in the garage was almost right again. *Knock, knock, knock,* I almost jumped out of my chair when you don't hear a certain sound for what was probably years at this point. I almost ran and grabbed my shotgun because I couldn't grab the other thing that was taking a vacation at another property, it couldn't have been Zach; we hardly communicated anymore and he gave up the surprise trips so as I walked to the door and considered not opening it. I didn't want to look to suspicious, mostly everyone up there knew I was a full timer there now even though I rarely got out public records are easy to find and get your hands on you want to do the research.

I took a few deep breaths and I was going to need an oxygen mask when I opened the door to see a Chestertown police car sitting in the driveway. For a small town, a large police force was not necessary but still needed law enforcement with the aid of the state troopers in the summertime to make sure the out-of-towners stayed in line.

"Good morning, sir, are you James Marshall?" bumbling.

"Yes, officer, that's me, how can I help you on this fine morning?"

"I'm Officer Whitlock and we are just doing a courtesy check on some of the properties of permanent owners around to make sure everything is okay."

A courtesy check?

We have been coming here for years and I am not sure we have ever had a courtesy check. Sure you would see a patrol car or a trooper car making the rounds on the main road from time to time but I had no recollection of them doing door to door checks. I bet he only came to my camp and then went back to the station, so I gladly offered that everything was nice and quiet at the good ole Marshall Camp and I would contact the department if I saw anything unusual.

To say my now sense of urgency was greatly elevated to the highest peak of the tallest mountain around the lake would have been the understatement of the year. I was going full ninja spy James Bond to secure the rolling pin *tonight*, no excuses. I tried closing my eyes and getting some rest as I had not slept well in a few days and quick trip to the bathroom and washing my face, my eyes were looking quite weary so I faded back in the chair, stewing and panicking over the visit by the officer in the morning, skipped lunch, skipped dinner. I would force myself to eat when I got back to the camp with the damn rolling pin. I waited until it was pretty dark this time as I now knew the line I had to take and get back to the camp. I raced out and through the woods and to the same spot I might as well as set up a little porch. I had been there so much more often than I should have been but it was my own damn fault, I just had to grab it and get the hell back to camp. I dug through and found a mini flashlight that we would use at the end of the dock for some night time fishing, so I would be able to point it squarely under the side of the camp and not out into the driveway. Get to the door, shimmy the side of the camp, grab down with my right hand, and back to the tree line and home to finally give myself a full meal. The car was parked in the driveway tonight but there didn't appear to be any lights on just what would appear would be a night light. Perfect, through the tree line and I make my move to the side door to get ready for my sweet victory when all of a sudden, I step closer to the door and the same motion light that was disabled on my previous visits now lit up the whole side of the camp. Sweating now, I figured I had twenty seconds to run and grab it by the time if someone saw the light came on and just figured it was an animal messing around the only problem was that some of the shine of the light went out into the driveway.

"Rolling pin secured, rolling pin secured," I signaled back to base camp, now I needed the extraction team to come get me before someone stumbled down the stairs and opened the side door and ventured outside. I tried to be quiet, stumbling back into the woods and knocked over the small woodpile that I used for cover earlier that same day and took two deep breaths before turning my head around to monitor if I was uncovered. I didn't hear any doors open and it didn't appear any new lights were on in the camp so worst case, someone may have glanced out the back window, in which case, I was not in direct view at that point as of yet and they may have just figured some tree branches fell or some animals were scrounging around for some food. I felt like I just won the gold medal in the one-hundred-meter dash, beating the fastest person alive with a breathtaking finish that made the crowd go wild with excitement, so I snuck around the trees and got back to my trail and two steps in twist; luckily, in all of our years playing sports, growing up, Zach and I remained pretty healthy, no major breaks of bones, the usual soreness and tweaks here and there, but no major damage. I didn't hear anything pop but it felt like someone just twisted my right leg like they were putting me in the figure four leg lock. The limp back to the camp took forever and it definitely wasn't as quiet as I was hoping for, I was hoping the mask would catch all of my swear words and grunts as I struggled to put any weight on the leg. I just about fell into the garage after getting the door open, threw my boots off, threw my clothes in the dryer with the mask, and limped inside with my gold medal to give it a soaking in the tub like it just played a grueling overtime football game. I didn't wash too many dishes because I wasn't using too many dishes so I nearly put half the bottle of dish soap in the sink and filled it up with hot water and dropped the rolling pin and went for a swim. I grabbed two bags of frozen veggies and went to the couch; one bag under my leg and one bag squarely on top, praying it was just a sprain. The rolling pin was cleaning so I could take the night off and get some rest and limp around the camp tomorrow.

Chapter 19
Rest in Place

The set back of the knee forced me to stay inside for at least a few weeks, which was fine by me and I was not going to be making a doctor trip. I was just going to wait this one out; as the temperature started dropping, I would rehab this one myself with stretching and icing at night and not going out at all. I only imagined how the conversation would go, "So, Jim, what did you do? Tried to bring back your youth on a hike or long run."

All the while me squirming on the exam table, "Yep, exactly, doc, ain't as young as I feel."

The only thing that snapped was the tree limb I got caught up on and nothing popped so he would have told me to do the same thing I was doing, "Rest it up and ice it and no more road races or on trails, that would be trickier than the normal path for several weeks."

Sold, I didn't need to set off any red flags to warrant another courtesy check by Officer Whitlock so staying in as the winter was now in full swing was fine by me.

Mobility started to improve slightly over the course of the next few weeks, chuckling by the back window, looking out at the frozen lake and being the age I am now; when we were younger, something this simple may have kept us out a day and we would have been racing around at one hundred miles an hour again. I needed to take this time to evaluate what I was going to do next. I could only see so many camps through the back window and couldn't gauge if everyone retreated back home before the first big snowfall. I wasn't going out with the limp, so I shuttered in place and ran on the supplies that I had stocked up on. Was the village still going to be crowded going into the new year, or would we be getting back to normal? That was the one question that burned in my mind. I would check in with family on the mantle and bookshelf to see how they were doing and that I was sorry and hoped they forgave me for what I now became, such a far cry from what the plans were years ago. I wept and could barely look at either of them so I collected them all and moved them to one of the spare bedrooms almost like what I would do with my winter and summer clothes when it was time to change wardrobes for the season.

The first big snowfall that was going to test my rehabilitating knee and I had to admit that I did a pretty good number on it; worse than I originally thought and was probably just the pure rush of adrenaline that I escaped outta there with the rolling pin that the severity was diminished. I opened the garage door and made sure there was fresh gas in the snowblower and fired her up. I still had a hitch in the old giddy up but overall, it was tolerable, which was encouraging news that I would be able to do it myself and not have to call someone just in case I needed to leave the cap for an emergency. First few paths back and forth were refreshing to get some fresh air and be active again and as I got through half of the drive, I started to look around and see if I could monitor any activity or lack thereof at camps in the surrounding area. While the exact camps may not of been visible what was visible was the smoke coming from whatever heating source a particular camp used and looking around instead of not seeing too much, I just pushed my head down and finished the driveway and set the snowblower back inside the garage and grabbed a fresh six pack from the fridge and went back inside.

Looking out at the frozen lake, steaming at the smoke signals, I saw while taking care of the driveway lit the inner fire and rage candle again and even a slight limp wouldn't prevent me from getting the trail clothes and boots in their proper place to take a stroll when the sun set and the village was nice in dark. I was going to head a different direction this time as my driveway was nice and clear and the main road had one lane completely clear, so there was an easy path to travel that would have been covered by morning or plowed over again by the town. It was slightly more of a gamble, I was aware, but I wasn't just the one sheltering in place through the winter usually, that's all you could do anyway. It's not like you could head to the beach, so you needed indoor activities to keep you busy. Up the driveway and a left-hand turn set me in the direction of the camp's smoke signal set me off and it looked like it was an easy entrance from the driveway to keep from being seen, no large windows in the front approaching the camp, just a front door with a light lit overhead. Perfect! I would have some light to help me around the camp. I approached the camp carefully as to get a sense of a good point of entry and go from there. A quick tour around the entirety of the camp,

I focused on a few spots that looked like they provide a good entry and exit point, The first around the back deck looked like a door of an extra bedroom with no lights on that I may be able to get open and get in but the downside was, it was on the opposite side of the camp so I would have to circle back around the front of the camp to get back to the driveway, and there was a sliding glass door on the back deck that I kept on the back burner around the rest of the exterior, that was it; three doors to choose from which one would give me the best prize like I was on *Let's Make a Deal* and I was sweating over which door was going to give me the most excitement. The exterior of the camp was your typical looking structure, two stories surrounded by trees, but one thing just pissed me off while looking at it, a yellow fucking front door, bright yellow, had to be some bright idea of a millennial to paint a door that color. That was it, the lock popped with the army knife again and entered through the front door and everyone was sleeping, using the anger from the yellow door after two bedroom visits, I left and hit the trail new trail back to the camp as the snow continued to fall and my knee feeling like someone just waved a magic wand over it.

A dose of ibuprofen and a swig of jack before bed and I was out like a baby, dreaming about that damn yellow door and smiling. Hopefully, the next owner changes the color. I sat quietly in the nice warm cabin, enjoying my beverages, and tried to muster up the willingness to break the cookbooks out again after the puzzles and solitaire were no longer able to hold my attention. I would get three quarters of the way through a fairly simple recipe and then just turn everything off and throw it outside for the raccoons or the winter birds to gather up the scraps when we would get our next cover of snow to head for the next smoke signal by a different path.

I could tell by the morning air that another snowstorm was coming so I turned into the camp and awaited for the snow to make its presence and took to the deck as my place of observation and trail scouting spot on a potential course over the next few days when a fresh coat was put down. Peering out across the snow-covered land and trees, trying to catch a glimpse at the strong smoke signal to plot the best trail. Bull's eye, a strong signal soaring above the trees, whatever they were using it was being used to its capacity, so I patiently waited for what I knew was coming. Not a lot accumulation, so I would be able to stay off the main road but just enough to provide a covering on the ground to make it a manageable trek through the woods as it couldn't have been that far away so I wasn't going to be straining my knee by walking a long distance to and from. I waited for night to fall and walked down the stairs of the deck and set my line through the woods to get to the new camp. This venture led me to the side of the camp with what looked like pretty level piece of land, which was somewhat unique as a lot of properties had some form of slope or incline or decline in one direction but anyways, that was a moot point as I would have been able to maneuver; albeit a little bit slower now, was still just as effective. Settling in next to a tree, near the camp, was one of the adrenaline rushes and solving the puzzle of how I would enter and exit successfully after trying to teach these people that they should have gone home or they should not have rented in my territory. I figured going in the front door this time, maybe, shouldn't be the best course of action, so I scoured a little bit harder and circled the camp twice to make sure I wasn't hastily making a decision on an entry point and I could use a little bit of discretion on this trip for God's sake or at this point, it was in the direction's sake and not heaven's sake, that's for damn sure. Usual set up, garage doors closed, front door, and this camp just had a door facing the back of the camp, no sliding glass door or anything like that, so I figured I'd give that one a check first and wouldn't ya know it, it was double rigged with a deadbolt. Back to square one at the tree and canvassing the grounds being that it was level two windows of regular size on the side of the camp not far off the ground that appeared to be in a bedroom or small office. It was tough to tell with the lights off and not wanting to just go ahead and shine a flashlight in there. Right window locked, come on, forgot to lock the window on the left after the last decent day to get some fresh air in the camps. It would happen especially with the older windows even just in our camp. Sam would yell at me if they were shut and not locked and I would scoff back, "Ain't nobody here to bother us, what's the problem?"

"Well, if there ain't a problem, why is there a shotgun locked out in the garage?"

Check and mate, yes, mam, the windows will be locked, and look at me now, searching for unopened windows, trying to bother some people. Left window locked; the knife didn't have a glass cutter on it so it was time for another gamble quite possibly more risky than the front door entry. *Smash,* found a nice spot in the pain by the lock and butted it with the end of the flashlight and the window was unlocked. Knee was healing but it was still not one hundred percent, so climbing through the window was not quite skillful or remotely athletic and wouldn't ya know it, first step on the ground, this God awful screeching snarl of a cat's meow. Alright, two for two, broken window and stepping on the cat, I was banking on something else being on inside the house the heating source definitely was so that had to add some blanket cover but I regrouped myself and prepared for the action coming to me and boy, was I right. I didn't have time to ask whether it was the glass breaking or the stupid cat in apparently its own bedroom. Zach and I had a few cats when we were growing up, Sam loathed them and swore them off as we were never going to own them. Alright, I wasn't going to argue to each their own but the door flung open to a man holding a decent size kitchen knife and he made the first lunge and a quick jab with the army knife to that same hand he was holding the knife, it dropped and it was grapple time like our Saturday and Sunday morning wrestling shows, which was probably better for my knee. I was able to subdue and constrict the airway. I didn't see any other lights come on and didn't hear any doors slam or phones ringing, so I quick searched the rest of the house to find a hiding spouse in the master bathroom. I am not sure how she didn't call the police in the middle of all that but there was no phone with her so she was eliminated to cover my tracks as I wiped down the areas of the wrestling match and the window I came in. I at least found a nice cover up for it and mozied on back to camp. I was considering adding some milestones to the rolling pin but after one lapse in judgment, leaving it at the one camp, that wouldn't be a wise decision like I was making a bunch of them these days but this was in fact a good one, so chalk it up on the good side! It felt like I slept for three days as my knee felt a little more limber and going into the new year was going to be a fresh start.

Chapter 20
Johnny Questions

We were now finally on the downslope of winter instead of riding the chairlift up winter mountain and I was ready to get my summer back. Heading into March, what would hope to only be maybe two or three snowfalls left with a few nice days breaking fifty degrees sprinkled in there to do the normal after winter check and gather any downed tree branches that would help get the first fires started and make sure no additional dock damage had been found and everything around the Marshall Camp looked to be in tip top shape with just the usual tidying up in order. The knee would flare up if I overdid it on a cleaning spree but it felt fine enough to power through it and it got enough rest to not need any additional attention.

My position at Landy's was technically still there if I wanted but I stopped requesting hours, even if just for a part-time gig, working with the public any longer wasn't going to fit into my charming personality that had now developed. No loss, I still had the means to keep the beer fridge stocked and heat through the winter, so why put myself through twenty to thirty hours of terror each week. I was going to enjoy this summer the way it used to be. I even brought the urns out of their winter bedroom and placed them back in their spots to get ready for the nice fresh air that would circulate through the camp. Spring cleaning, what a glorious time, the trail clothes that had become so useful in the winter still stashed out in the garage got a final wash and placed nicely in my closet for a summer nap and my warmer weather hiking clothes took their place and the boots got a good scrubbing to get back to our normal trails and walks around the lake.

A nice spring morning; the sun shining, I decided to take my freshly brewed coffee out onto the deck and breathe in some of the fresh air and as I am sitting down blaring siren, the roaring sounds of a fire truck seemingly going at the speed of light. Looking up, I didn't really see any unusual smoke that would signal distress, just the heat that was still on at the surrounding camps. You would get this type of response from time to time. Things happen, you know, so I didn't really pay much attention to it and just enjoyed the view of the lake and my delicious "death wish" coffee that was now the only coffee that I drank as everything else just tasted like warm water. Back inside, after the last drop of the first cup was finished, I was enroute for more since one cup was never enough. Not that I really needed it, but it just tasted so damn good and my phone was positioned on the counter and it really was simply a paper or puzzle weight at this point although Zach would always scold me if it wasn't turned on for a period in case someone needed to get a hold of me. I downloaded a local news app when I was actually still paying attention and gave a damn to the local news and almost forgot I even downloaded it but this update was one I was not going to ignore.

"Dead body found on local beach."

Shit! The tie job must have snapped. I thought it was strong enough to hold a boat at a dock but the force must have pushed the body away. All winter in the frozen lake would take some time to investigate and everything inside the camp was spot clean so, maybe, just chalk it up to a couple not used to bunking together for too long and they grew to hate each other and he or she just simply had enough. I wasn't as concerned as I guess I should have been by this news update. Ice fishing was also a pretty popular activity by the locals as well, so did someone take a gamble by going out on ice that wasn't quite ready yet after having a few too many beverages. This was a pretty big deal for a small town like this. Someone dying in their camp, that's one thing; a body washing up on the shore of one of the public beaches, that's a completely different ballgame. I even turned on the local news where they had their field reporter live at the beach with local and state police cars filling the parking lot and instead of the caution ropes that lined the entrance to the sand, it was roped off with the yellow caution tape signaling a crime scene. Seeing all the flashing lights and the ambulance getting ready to load the stretcher with the black bag ready to take a drive to the coroner's office for examination, I moved up in my chair to see what the local police chief was going to say when he came on camera and then I saw my buddy, Officer Whitlock, standing in the background, holding the perimeter as the nossie nellies started to flock to the beach like a flock of birds coming back to the lake after their winter vacation.

"We don't have any answers at this time and the investigation is under review. We would like to ask the people to stay calm as we are doing everything in our power with help from the New York state troopers to keep everyone safe."

Blah, blah, blah, and I clicked the television off. Back out to the deck, with my second cup of coffee, and I took a nice big breath of the morning air and enjoyed the view of the lake.

I could only imagine the locals freaking out and the out-of-towners panicking over breakfast about the body washing up at the shore and maybe this would be a blessing and help speed along the departure of some of the residents and get things back to normal a little bit quicker. Was the charter going to form a Pinecone Watch Group now to keep an eye out for unusual activity? Would they upgrade to security systems and motion lights and dial Officer Whitlock every time a chipmunk or bird flew onto their deck?

"Officer Whitlock, this is Roger Aiken, and I think a piece of wood is approaching my camp and looks to be armed, can you send a squad car?"

I missed my calling to be a comedian; at least I could laugh at my own jokes. *If you didn't think your own jokes were funny, then what's the freaking point?* I always thought.

The afternoon was drenched in sun and although the temperature was barely around fifty when you have struggled to hit thirty for months on end, a fifty-degree day could feel like seventy, so I brought a chair down to the dock and just sat down and enjoyed the beauty. I really lost track of time as I was numb in the chair and was nice and peaceful until I heard that voice again from up by the camp.

"Mr. Marshall? Hello? Are you around?"

For Pete's sake or whatever his first name was, what now? I figured it was time to get up and head back to the camp anyways, so I met him about halfway and exchanged pleasantries.

"What brings ya over, Mr. Whitlock?"

"I don't know if you saw the news this morning but a body was found on one of the public beaches."

"Oh, no, how terrible, doesn't happen often around these parts."

"Exactly, so this is a little bit more of a cautionary visit we're making to just tell residents to be more vigilant in monitoring their surroundings and report anything unusual."

"Of course, officer, thank you for the heads up and thank you for all of your hard work and stay safe out there."

I handed him the dumb card and escorted him back to the driveway. I glanced to the left as we were getting ready to make the turn to the driveway and noticed him looking down at my knee area and figured he wasn't admiring my nice jeans. Was he going to ask the question or should I just jump out in front of it and squash his little detective brain stop in its tracks?

"Not as young as I once was, used to be football games that would give me soreness, now cleaning up after the winter gives me aches and pains."

167

"Get that rested up, Mr. Marshall, need to be ready for the summer fun."

There was definitely going to be a watch group, no doubt in my mind. After this visit, everyone with their safety vests, someone taking watch each night, a patrol car may be making the rounds each night. I dare not ask if they suspected anything suspicious or how they were investigating it exactly. I was going to quietly head back into camp and mind my p's and q's until they determined a cause or came to a resolution.

Several days passed and the beach still taped off and I flipped on the news to see if there was any update and wouldn't ya know it, accidental drowning after falling through an ice fishing hole, bang, bang, did you ever do a celebration using finger guns?

I was like I just hit the lottery. The caution tape taken down and the panic o meter dropping slightly back to a normal level. You know they had to expect this uptick of activity since there was far more people here than usual, so there was going to be more unusual activity, maybe if they weren't gloating about how business was and paid a closer eye on the volume of random people still around a sacrifice in security would not have been made. People doing dumb stuff that they weren't used to, venturing out onto the lake when they barely know how to walk on a sidewalk. I felt bad for the person, I truly did, but a lake 101 course should have been offered up to these people on how to act.

Time to push the snowblower to the back of the garage and sweep the front of the camp and driveway of any limbs I missed through the winter and any pinecones that were trespassing. I always worked toward the road starting at the garage for some reason, quirky trend, I guess, but it was nice to get to the top of the slight incline and admire the nice view of a clean driveway and get a look at the lake over the top of the camp it was always refreshing and a welcome of the new season. Car tires made a certain noise on the road depending on how fast they were traveling; if a car was taking its time and going nice and slow, it was a slight crackle of the stones and dirt combination with any foliage that may have made its way onto the path. If someone was just trying to be an ass or in a hurry, it sounded like a race at a dirt track race and it was more like a spewing of dirt and rocks sound. This was the first nice slow pace and the ground just crackled beneath the tread of the tires and I turned around and the same white car with green trim and lights on top. Officer Whitlock riding in on his white chariot of peace, was this a stopping visit or a passing by the grounds visit? I guess I would soon find out and turned out, he was just passing through to do a loop and monitor activity, so I tipped my real old Mets ball cap to him and watched him drive on by before curiously spitting in the road before making the turn back down the driveway and into the camp.

Pacing back and forth in the camp at sunset was usually an exciting time as someone would be down by the firepit getting ready for our evening adventure and laughing with company. Now I was pacing, trying to calm my thoughts down when I turned to the deck and agreed, *not tonight*, we weren't to summer daylight hours, yet so I wouldn't have to wait as long but I was heading to the first camp I saw and that feeling of plotting the course by a tree before jumping into action that I thought I was going to be able to subdue until the results of the lake population were either seen or gossiped about. The spot by the door was set to go and the sky was pitch dark and I set out at a furious pace to the nearest camp and parked it by a tree just about twenty yards away from a firepit area and smoke rising from the firepit that looked like a fresh fire going on with chairs and blankets still sitting on them. I was smiling under the mask as I was waiting for the chairs to be occupied, bouncing my left leg ready to take off like a sprinter, hearing the gun sound in his or her attempt to win a gold medal. I was getting anxious and I wanted to pounce and wanted to do it now. They had just sat down and with it so dark and my eyesight not as strong any longer, I couldn't make out if all four chairs were occupied and everyone was in the rightful place. I had a decision to make wait it out or risk them calling it a night and missing my opportunity. What felt like fifteen minutes, I pounced swiftly through the trees and quickly counted three chairs occupied. Perfect, deep sigh into the mask as the fire raged. I placed another log onto the fire for good measure because it was a nice fire and retreated back into the woods and back to camp for a nice nightcap; three parts jack, one part coke, and a nice peaceful night's sleep.

What the hell is that noise and where is it coming from at? I assumed it was very early in the morning; the first time I was upset at being up so early as I was in a deep slumber. I had no idea where the noise was coming from, so I stumbled into the kitchen and it was my phone ringing. I almost forgot how to answer it and didn't even recognize the ringtone. Zach or Sam must have programmed it to some goofy sound when I wasn't looking.

"Hey, good morning, Jim, how are you doing?"

"I'm tired, who is this calling so early?"

"Officer Whitlock here, was just wondering if I could bug ya with a few questions?"

"Sure thing, officer, let me just shake the cobwebs in my tired brain and I'd love to answer anything you need to ask."

"Did you do anything fun last night, Jim?"

"Unfortunately, officer, my fun activities stopped a long time ago. I just enjoy the solitude of this beautiful camp."

"Did you happen to take a walk or a hike at any point yesterday?"

"It did cross my mind but I actually dozed off after dinner and stayed up a little late watching TV instead, which is why I wasn't awake already when you called"

"Great, that's it, Mr. Marshall, I do appreciate your time this morning."

A phone call?

Alright, maybe they just needed to save some of the gas for the residents and the extra people were staying at the lake. Maybe he was doing phone duty today and selling calendars to raise money. At least we were building a report now and it wasn't one of the trooper vehicles making the rounds and phone calls yet. He was just doing his duty for the community.

Chapter 21
The Untied Knot

Watching the local news was now like trying to watch the stock market during trading hours but instead of watching for the hottest stocks, I was checking for reports on how populated the camp still was. Surely in light of recent events, the volume had to be sharply down and back to normal and I would wait for the live on-site shots at various places and hope for an update with a local business to provide key information one way or another on what we were dealing with. They seemed to be pretty somber and low-key vibes with no direct questions to give me a straight answer, so I would have to wait it out and huff and puff on the deck looking for smoke signals and try and gauge the activity level again as the warmer weather was approaching and my desire to retire the clothes in the garage and just take a nice long walk around the lake.

"We now interrupt the scheduled programming and a breaking news update."

Well, this was an event that I could surely count on one hand for our local news station. The same crowd that appeared by the beach when the body was found was positioned by the police headquarters and when I heard the update, I dropped my coffee mug.

"The Chestertown police again, with the help of the New York State Troopers, are now investigating a possible homicide that occurred the other evening at one of the camps in our town."

A fucking homicide? How? I checked the spot by the door and everything was where it needed to be and I went through the checklist probably a dozen times and I quickly grabbed everything and buried them deep in the closet as all I had to do to put them in plain sight was open the door and you could see them clear as day. I thought I was going to break the rocking chair. I was rocking back and forth so fast out of sheer panic. I needed to get some air before I was going to get sick and the slight rain drops that were falling felt quite refreshing as I headed to the dock and plopped down in the chair. Mind racing, *all right, all right, get your head right. I already talked with Whitlock and gave him my straight answers.*

Would back up come in the form of a trooper visit? Maybe his boss? I was going to play the solitary confinement game and reputation that frankly with the new delivery services, I wasn't seen too much in town and I certainly didn't have any open lines of communication with anybody. The trails through the woods, they are extremely popular, and would have been more so now because there were more people using them. I was talking myself off the proverbial ledge. Did you ever talk yourself into something so confidently whether it was right or wrong you had a zig to every zag and no matter what you were going to be at ease with your reasoning? That's where I was, well, and also with a long swig straight from the Jack bottle to calm the nerves down. Looking at the bottle, I almost kissed it, thanks to drinking this beautiful stuff. I had received my delivery that day around dinner time, perfect, timestamp of someone else actually seeing me and me not going off of my word, visual proof. I would always hand the delivery person a ten or twenty to show my gratitude, so there would be a brief interaction after they dropped the beautiful stuff in front of the garage. See, talking yourself into believing your reasoning and explanations were enough to garner a defense and a sense of righteousness in any situation. I turned a few swigs into making it a half a bottle adventure sitting out on the back deck to suppress my anxiety and worry.

Checking the weather for the forecast of April 19th was very pleasant as it looked like I was going to be able to get a nice walk in around the lake and take a camp count or a busy attendance to see if everyone made their way back home and we were back to normal for the summer season. Up the driveway and first step onto the road, the same car approaching. I just figured he was going to keep driving by for the usual drive through the village, so I kept walking on my path, eager to get a sense of traffic but this time, he braked and opened his door as I was approaching the car.

"Perfect, just the man I was looking for."

Me turning around like he had to be talking to someone else, right?

"I don't blame ya, Jim, great day for a walk!"

"Why it sure is, officer, I hope you have a good day."

"Jim, I'm going to need you to come down to the station with me and just answer some questions we need to ask you, okay?"

"More questions? You called me the other day with questions, too, weren't those sufficient?"

"They were perfect, but we would just like to bring ya in for a few more."

Deep breath in, deep breath out, it was going to be okay. I retraced the explanation from the other night as I was getting in the front seat of the squad car, liquor delivery, early nap, thought about going on a hike, stayed up late watching TV, slept in. Patting myself on the back as we walked into the police station through a side door and into a private room.

"Can I get ya any water or a coffee? Do you need anything to eat, Jim?"

"A water would be good."

"How come I'm in here and not out in the main area with everyone else?"

"Don't worry, Jim, we have someone that will be right in and just wants to ask you a few questions."

Someone? Great, okay.

Another silent recap in my head, I was going to be fine. This was initial questioning. Whitlock didn't put me in the back of the car, they knew I was a longtime resident and I was going to be fine. The door swung open and they entered the room.

"Jim, I would like you to meet Detective O'Reilly, she just wants to ask you the questions this time."

"Mr. Marshall, I'm heading the homicide investigation. I am sure you are well aware about now and we just wanted to ask a few follow up questions on your whereabouts and activity on the night of April 13th?"

"Sure, but I already provided Officer Whitlock with that information previously, Detective O'Reilly."

"Please, Jim, feel free to call me Rebecca, could you just share with us your activity on that night please, the 13th?"

"I was in my camp, planned on taking a walk after my liquor delivery arrived but I dozed off and woke up later than I wanted to get started, so I turned the TV on and just stayed in."

"Did you know the people who were killed, Jim?"

"No, I did not, I am not exactly a socialite anymore and if Officer Whitlock hasn't told you, I mind to myself and stay at my camp."

"Of course, you do, Jim, from what Officer Whitlock tells me about the camp, you have a beautiful property."

Tells her about the camp, alright, he just had to give her the basic general background scoop on the people near the area, pretty standard operating procedure.

"Jim, we thank you for coming down here on this nice day. Officer Whitlock will drop you off back at your camp now."

Heading back to camp, I didn't want to be in the vehicle any longer, so I had him drop me off a few miles away from the camp, so I could get my walk in. I let him know this was my plan anyways before I went to the station and I was going to walk away since it was so nice out and I needed to stretch the winter out of my legs. Was I the only one being brought in for these questions? I would think like before they would just gather any info from people calling in or going door to door of surrounding camps. A shake of the head and plowing forward, I wasn't even looking around for what my intended purpose of this walk was going to be, it might as well have looked like Disney World around here and I would have been looking at the pavement with some quick glances for traffic and turns to the lake if I hear a splash. I enjoyed the rest of the afternoon out on the back deck, checking on the TV to see if there were any updates coming in about the investigation and it was good the TV really hadn't been used much prior because now it was kept on day and night.

This was unchartered waters and couldn't tell you if there ever was in fact a production like this going on in the town so I didn't even know if Detective O'Reilly was from the Chestertown department or brought in from somewhere else. I just knew I didn't want to keep the conversation going any longer than she wanted to. It was a waiting game now and who knew how long they would take to conclude their investigation but I was hunkered down at the friendly confines of the Marshall Camp and not looking through

177

bars. Grabbed a handful of beers from the fridge and brought them to the deck and opened two at a time as I wandered helplessly into the chair wondering why it all went so wrong and how it should have been. Sip of beer and shake of the head, need to get those negative thoughts out right now. I can't be heading down magnolia lane like I am going to get caught right now. I'll be fine, just ride it out and they won't find anything and O'Reilly will head back to whatever big city department she was brought in from.

The days were moving at slow pace as I would frantically wait for a breaking news update and the normal updates first thing in the a.m., noontime, and then the 6 p.m. news, the superstars had to be getting close to get this thing wrapped up shortly right. A week of sitting in front of the TV like we used to do watching *Saturday Night Live* or a sporting event, I was waiting for the news to break that someone was taken into custody well knowing that was a long shot but they did rule the beach body an ice fishing accident but I doubt they had any assistance on that one. I was bringing the beer bottles to the recycling bin in the garage with the door open to get some of the winter smell out and after placing them in the bin and turning around to head back inside the passenger and driver side door of Whitlock's car open, Officer Whitlock and Detective O'Reilly.

"Well, detective, I hope it doesn't disappoint from what our fine officer described to you."

"I wish I was here to explore and look around Jim," as she gave a quick nod to Officer Whitlock.

"James Marshall, you have the right to remain silent," and this time, I wasn't going to be so lucky to sit in the front seat of the car. We entered the same door as last time and even went to the same room, but I wasn't offered any treats this time and I needed to get my shit together and quickly.

"Jim, were you at the crime scene that night?"

"Again, no, I was not, I was at my camp."

"Jim, I am going to ask one more time. Why were you at that camp that night?"

"I wasn't at their camp. I don't go anywhere anymore."

"Fine, that's the story you're sticking to, what if I told you that the whole family wasn't outside when they were murdered?"

No, no, how could that be? I waited there patiently just for that purpose that couldn't be the truth. She was just playing me to get me to confess. There was no way someone was inside the whole time I was canvassing the fire pit to ensure just for that purpose. When I finally made it to the fire pit, even the glance at one of the empty chairs just had a blanket folded just in case someone else needed but there was nothing there that indicated personal belongings.

While the killer brutally attacked her family, this brave fourteen-year-old quietly gathered the best observation she could before retreating back into the camp and escaping to a nearby camp to call the authorities, she noticed one very specific trait about this person. They had a slight limp, or a hitch in their step heading back into the woods, thinking the job was complete. Detective O'Reilly went on to explain as I peered helplessly to Officer Whitlock standing in the corner of the room.

"I will ask you again, Jim, why were you there that night?"

"What does this have to do with me? Why am I under arrest?"

"Murder."

"Oh my lord, I can't murder anyone, let's not be silly now."

"Jim, you are not going anywhere and are being held until further notice. Just one final question before we put you in your new office for the time being, *why*?"

"I would like to exercise my right to an attorney before I say anything further, please."

I knew the answer to her question. It was quite the simple one honestly. I could not say it out loud so I thought it to myself in a nice stern manor, *End the laughter.*

CPSIA information can be obtained
at www.ICGtesting.com
Printed in the USA
BVHW042119211221
624666BV00013B/511